THE PICTURE
THAT MADE
TIME FLY

THE PICTURE THAT MADE TIME FLY

Sheila Harries

Pont

Published in 2015 by Pont Books, an imprint of
Gomer Press, Llandysul, Ceredigion, SA44 4JL

ISBN 978 1 84851 969 5
ISBN 978 1 84851 970 1 (ePUB)
ISBN 978 1 84851 971 8 (Kindle)

A CIP record for this title is available from the British Library.

This book is published with the financial support of the
Welsh Books Council.

Printed and bound in Wales at
Gomer Press, Llandysul, Ceredigion

For my grandchildren –
Gethin, Osian, Siân, Isaac,
Vincent and Orla –
who all enjoy reading
or being read to.

Chapter 1

THE DARK PICTURE

'Right, is everyone here?'

Miss Jones cast a rapid glance around the group of children as they shuffled, fidgeted and poked around inside their back-packs. The girls were giggling and whispering, the boys giving each other furtive shoves and kicks. Miss Jones frowned at them with a look that said 'Behave!'

'Where's Rhys? Why is that boy never where he's supposed to be? Megan, you know your way around the museum. Will you go back to the art gallery and tell him to hurry up? We're going down to the natural history galleries next. We have to meet a museum guide there, so we'll be just by the door.'

'Yes, Miss.'

She hoisted her bag onto her shoulder and turned to go back through the picture galleries to look for him. Rhys had been her best friend for a long time and she had often had to get him out of scrapes on their many 'adventures'. She didn't mind that.

Her class was on a visit to the National Museum in Cardiff. Megan had been there several times before with her grandparents, who lived nearby in Penarth, so she was quite familiar with its elegant staircases and grand galleries – unlike the rest of her class, who had travelled from Aberystwyth to spend three days in the capital, some for the first time

Their visit had started that morning with the paintings and they'd walked through rooms full of old portraits of serious looking men and haughty ladies. They had seen landscapes of mountains and castles, and then gone into a long gallery where there were many canvasses in ornate frames which Miss Jones said had been painted by Italian and Dutch artists.

Megan retraced her footsteps back past these paintings and looked into the room called 'The Welsh Landscape'. She spotted Rhys at the far end. He was standing in front of a large picture painted in dark oils and surrounded by a heavy gilded frame.

'Come on, Rhys, Miss Jones is waiting. Why are you still staring at that picture?'

'Well, the grown–ups in here seem to spend ages just staring at the pictures as if they're in a magic trance, so I thought I'd do the same and see what happened. Anyway, I really like this one'

'I wonder why the painter wanted to paint such a gloomy scene,' Megan said. 'You can hardly see the boats in it.' She peered at the label next to the painting. It said: 'Entrance to Cardiff Docks, Evening, by Lionel Walden, 1897.'

'A very interesting image of Cardiff all the same.'

The voice that came from close behind them made the children jump and turn round. A tall, elderly man with wispy white hair and twinkling blue eyes was standing there, although Megan was sure that a moment before there had been no-one else in the gallery. He was dressed in a rather old-fashioned looking black coat and had an identity badge hanging on a ribbon around his neck.

'I see that you have your bags with you ready for a journey. I hope you have some victuals to sustain you,' he said, pointing to their backpacks.

Megan gave him a half-smile and started to walk away uneasily. Victuals? What were they? she thought. And why did she need them? She caught Rhys' eye and sensed his uneasiness.

'Come on,' she said. 'Let's go and find the others or we'll be in trouble.'

'Oh, I think the picture deserves a longer viewing, young lady,' said the man, with an encouraging gesture inviting them to look again. 'It has a certain interest, I feel. You see, Cardiff was a very different place in Victorian times when it was painted. It was the powerhouse of the world, sending its ships with coal and steel to far–flung places, its chimneys belching out smoke and its furnaces blazing night and day. It was one of the busiest ports in the world.'

Rooted to the spot, Megan and Rhys found themselves listening carefully to the man's dramatic words. He continued.

'But what of the people? There are children like you two living there, you know – many who are poor, helpless, neglected, mistreated. I feel that two strong, healthy, intelligent young people such as you, young lady, and your friend here, could lend a hand to some of them.'

Megan stared at the mysterious man and frowned slightly.

'What do you mean?' she asked. She had, of course, been told not to talk to strangers but this man seemed to be an official museum guide, so surely it was alright. 'The people who lived when this picture was painted are all dead now, aren't they?'

'Well, young lady, you would be surprised. Sometimes the past is closer than you think,' the man said, with a smile.

Rhys was beginning to look worried now.

'Come on,' he muttered, pulling her arm. 'We'd better go or Miss Jones will be really mad.' And he whispered under his breath, 'He must be a bit of a nutter.' He glanced nervously at the black-coated figure. There was no-one else around. Even the sounds of footsteps and voices had faded. It was as if they were suspended in a silent bubble.

'Why don't you take a closer look at the painting, Megan?' the man urged, noting her slight hesitation. 'Pictures can be very powerful forces, you know – a sort of bridge to the past.'

Megan shifted nervously. Perhaps Rhys was right and the man was a little mad. Or perhaps it was one of those tricks grown-ups play on you in museums to make things like boring paintings seem more interesting – to make things 'come to life'. In spite of himself, Rhys had walked back as well and was standing at Megan's side again. They both felt their eyes drawn irresistibly towards the picture.

'We really need to go and find the others,' Megan murmured, without taking her eyes off it.

But the more they stared at the painting, the less capable they felt of tearing themselves away. They were mesmerized by the reflections on the rippling water and the tall masts, silhouetted by the cloud of steam from the paddle-boat that was just leaving the crowded dockside. They could hear the shouts of the bystanders and the blast of the boat's horn.

The guide's voice seemed to come from a great distance behind them.

'Don't be frightened. I know that you are resourceful and imaginative children. I am sure that you will manage ...'

And with that the sound of his voice faded away completely and an immense roaring noise surrounded them.

As they felt themselves being drawn towards the painting, they instinctively grabbed hold of one another.

'What's happening?' Megan felt the floor slipping away from her and made one last attempt to turn back, before they were both sucked into a whirling vortex.

Chapter 2

CARDIFF DOCKS

The air rushed past her and the walls and floor of the gallery disappeared. She felt a rough, stony surface under her feet and a blast of damp air in her face. She could see nothing around her for a moment but as she blinked and her eyes grew more accustomed to the darkness, she could make out the shape of tall masts, the looming bulk of buildings, and here and there the flicker of wavering lights. Megan let go of Rhys' sweatshirt but Rhys was still holding on to her arm, his fingers tightly clenched.

'Ouch, let go,' she said, trying to shake his hand off. She peered at him in the gloom and realized that he had lost his usual bounce. He looked as if he had just been hit by a very large hammer.

'What happened there?' he stammered, still clutching Megan's arm. He stared around him, wide-eyed. 'This is the scene that was in that dark picture. Don't tell me that we're inside it. That's impossible. Is this some sort of virtual reality thing that the museum has put in for visitors?'

He suddenly became aware that he was still clinging on to Megan and hastily took his hand away.

'It's very good,' he said, rather shakily, as a burly man pushed past him, carrying a heavy sack on his shoulders, 'but I think they ought to warn you when it's going to happen, like they do on TV when there's going to be something frightening on. It might give some old person a heart-attack.'

'No, Rhys,' Megan replied slowly, taking in the bustling night time scene. 'I think that we really are in the picture. We seem to be standing on the dock-side. Look there are the boats. We must be in Cardiff in Victorian times.'

Rhys laughed in a rather artificial way.

'Don't be stupid, Meg,' he said. 'You can't make me believe that. I'm not a complete idiot.'

'Well, remember what that strange man said – something about the past being closer than you think and about helping someone? Don't you think that it all seems a bit too real for virtual reality?'

She tapped her foot on the stones under their feet and took a deep breath of the clammy night air with its fishy, sea-weedy smell mixed with a pungent aroma of smoke and coal dust.

'We shouldn't have spoken to that old weirdo. He's messed with your brain. How did he know your name?'

'He must have heard you say it, I suppose. Anyway, it's only because Miss Jones sent me back to look for you that I'm here. You could have been sucked into the picture by yourself.'

'Except that I wouldn't have spoken to that old man if I'd been by myself. You're the one who answered him.'

'Well, it's stupid standing here arguing. We seem to be starting on the biggest adventure we've ever had and it's not just one we've made up. We need to think what to do, but first I think we need to move away from here before those people see us.'

The crowd of dark figures appeared to be watching the boats and no-one had noticed the two children so far,

'No.' Rhys' face looked very pale in the dim light and his voice was shaking. 'Let's just find the button to press to go back to the museum. I don't like it very much here.'

'There's no button to press.' Megan peered around in the semi-darkness.

'So how do we get home?' Rhys couldn't keep the note of rising panic from his voice.

Megan thought hard for a reassuring answer. 'I'm not sure,' she said, slowly. 'But perhaps it's a bit like a computer game – now that we're in, perhaps we have to perform various tasks before we can get back out.'

'You're talking nonsense, Meg.' Rhys shivered. 'I must admit it's very realistic, though.' He took his back-pack off and started to scrabble around inside, trying to tip it towards the pale, flickering light of a nearby lamp.

'What are you doing?'

'Looking for my mobile. Then we can phone for help.'

He pressed the button, waiting for the logo to appear.

Nothing.

He tried again.

'Oh no – it won't come on! But I'm sure I charged it.'

'Of course it won't come on. It hasn't been invented yet. If we're inside the painting we're in Victorian times.' Megan sounded exasperated.

'Hello, what do we have here?' A slurred voice right beside them made them both jump.

'What have you kids been thieving then? Show us what you've got.'

Chapter 3

DANGER

A rough hand shot out of the darkness and made a grab for Rhys's arm. There was a reek of alcohol, tobacco and sweat, and a man's leering, unshaven face swayed before their eyes. Megan pulled Rhys away from his grasp and began to run.

'Come on, we need to hide somewhere,' she urged. Rhys followed, hugging his back–pack to his chest. She could hear the man behind them, cursing drunkenly as he stumbled along.

She looked around frantically and decided to make for the dark buildings on the dockside. She could just make out a brick wall and an unlit doorway, and they slid quickly into the shadows, listening for their pursuer. But they had been too fast for the man and he had given up the chase. Panting, they came to a halt and leaned against the door, to catch their breath.

'We shall have to be more careful,' Megan whispered. 'We'd better try and keep away from people until we can find someone we can trust.'

In a daze Rhys followed Megan meekly as she walked along in the shadow of the buildings which looked like warehouses. They could see the gleam of crisscrossing railway tracks opposite and the shimmer of light on a stretch of water.

'I don't know where you're going. We're getting further and further away from the place in the picture. This is stupid,' muttered Rhys.

'Oh, come on. Don't be so bad-tempered. You always say that you want a real adventure.'

'Shut up, Meg!' Rhys groaned. 'We are going to be in such mega-trouble when we get back to the gallery. Miss Jones will be furious that we've kept everyone waiting.'

Megan sighed. 'I think we've got more to worry about than Miss Jones. Like how exactly we're going to get back?' She put a hand on Rhys' arm. 'Come on,' she said, 'let's not fall out. We need to work this out together. We'll find somewhere to sit down and think what to do and we can eat our chocolate bars from our packed lunch.'

'Are you sure that this is Cardiff? I don't remember anything like this,' Rhys said.

'Well, it said it was Cardiff on the label by the painting and if it's the time when the picture was painted, of course it's going to look different.'

'And it smells horrible,' Rhys continued, wrinkling his nose as he passed a pile of steaming horse manure on the cobbles. 'This must be a really bad dream – I wish I could wake up.'

'Well, you can't,' snapped Megan. She had raised her voice without thinking and roused a guard dog somewhere behind one of the walls. There was an outburst of frantic barking and the rattle of chains then a menacing low growl.

They hurried on until they had left the sound of the dog behind.

Suddenly, Megan stopped.

'Look,' she said, 'that gate's not closed. Perhaps we can hide in there.'

'But there could be anything inside – another guard dog, for example. You do have some crazy ideas,' muttered Rhys, grumpily.

'Well, you don't seem to have any ideas at all,' retorted Megan, feeling just a little more scared than she dared show.

She was already pushing open the gate, cautiously. She could make out a yard and what looked like a pile of straw bales to one side. She pulled Rhys inside and behind the bales. There was a distinctive smell of horses and they could hear a stamping of hooves and the snorting, snuffling noise of animals munching. Across the yard, they could see a faint, bobbing light and hear someone whistling.

'There you go, my beauties, nos da,' a man's voice said and they watched as a lantern carried by a dark figure bobbed its way to the gate. There was a clash as it was pulled to, and the unmistakeable sound of a key turning in a lock, before the sound of footsteps faded away along the street.

Now, there was no way out.

Chapter 4

ASLEEP ON THE HAY

'Great,' said Rhys, 'Now we're locked in here.'

'But that means that we shall be safe until morning. We can find ourselves some straw or hay to sit on and we may be able to get some sleep. We can't do anything before it gets light anyway.'

Megan peeped inside the stable. There was no light but there seemed to be two horses in their stalls and she could make out a wooden ladder which went up to a hay–loft.

'Come on Rhys, in here,' she said.

'There are probably mice and rats,' Rhys protested as he followed Megan up the ladder but she ignored him and settled herself down in the hay.

'This is quite comfortable really,' she said. 'Now let's have our chocolate bars. We'd better keep our sandwiches until tomorrow morning.'

'I'm never going to be able to sleep,' sighed Rhys, after they had finished their snack. 'And we can't even play I-Spy because all I can spy is darkness and hay!'

'What about that a, b, c game – I'll start. Welsh towns, Aberystwyth.'

'Bangor,' said Rhys wearily.

'Cardiff.'

They continued through Animals, Birds, Food and Countries, and Megan was just trying unsuccessfully to remember a country beginning with V when she realized that Rhys had not said anything for the last few minutes. Peering closer, she found that he was fast asleep. 'Well, I'll just have to carry on by myself,' she thought, but before she reached X she had dozed off too.

They were awoken by the sound of the yard gates being unlocked, and sat bolt upright, startled and confused. It was still dark.

'Oh no,' Rhys muttered, 'we're still here. I thought it might all have been a dream.'

'We'd better go,' whispered Megan. 'Someone must have come to fetch the horses. We need to get out of the gate while it's open.'

They scrambled down the ladder. There was a light in what seemed to be the harness room and they could hear a metallic chink and the shuffling of heavy boots. The gate looked as if it had been left ajar.

'Let's run for it now,' said Megan.

'Hey! Where did you varmints come from? Stop!'

The ostler had spotted them, and he dropped his brushes and bucket with a clang on the stone flags. With seconds to spare, the children made it out of the gate and ran at full tilt along the road and round the corner. They didn't stop for breath until they were well away from the stables.

The sky was beginning to lighten now. They continued at a slower pace, keeping close to the wall until it came to a sudden end at a triangle of rough land, covered with long grass and small straggly bushes around the ruins of an old building.

'We'll stop here and eat some of our sandwiches, shall we?' Megan said. Her mother had always told her that she should start the day with a nourishing breakfast for energy, and it seemed as if she might need a good deal of energy to get through the day ahead. 'We can sit behind one of those piles of bricks and no-one will see us.'

Rhys followed her and watched as she squatted down and pulled out her packed lunch. She seemed remarkably calm and well-organized as she unwrapped a sandwich.

He was just about to open his own back-pack when, out of nowhere, a small, dark shape hurtled into Megan, making her topple sideways and cry out in surprise.

Chapter 5

AN UNEXPECTED MEETING

The figure rose up and seemed to fly through the air as Rhys' back-pack caught it fair-and-square and knocked it into a nearby tangle of brambles. There was a squeal of pain, then it struggled to its feet and showed itself to be a small, thin boy with tousled hair and ragged clothes. He made as if to run away but Rhys and Megan, who were larger and more bulky than he was, were blocking his escape and the boy's eyes were drawn to the sandwich that Megan still held in her hand. He raised his head to stare at her with large, dark eyes that seemed to fill his pale face.

'Who are you?' Megan asked. He continued to look at her fearfully and did not seem to understand, so she tried some Welsh. 'Pwy wyt ti? Beth yw dy enw di?'

The boy looked even more scared but he could not resist another longing glance at the sandwich.

'Are you hungry?' Megan tried and, still getting no answer, she broke a piece off the sandwich and handed it to him.

He raised it to his nose, sniffing a little suspiciously,

then crammed it into his mouth, chewing and swallowing rapidly.

'He really is starving,' exclaimed Megan.

'What are doing, giving him your sandwich?' Rhys sounded horrified. 'He tried to rob you. He might have a knife or something.'

'He doesn't look very scary,' said Megan, 'just really skinny and frightened.'

'What's your name?' she tried again and then, pointing at each of them in turn, 'Megan, Rhys'. She poked the boy gently in the chest.

'Luigi,' he said, swallowing the last piece of bread and licking his lips so as not to lose any crumbs.

'Luigi – that's an Italian name,' said Megan.

The boy nodded eagerly. 'Si, italiano,' he said.

Rhys sighed. Having seen Megan's sandwich he suddenly felt really hungry but he was reluctant to get his food out while the boy was still cowering there, staring at them.

'Let's get away from here and find somewhere else to eat,' he said, shifting uneasily.

But Megan was still preoccupied with the boy. She took out another sandwich and offered it to him.

'Do you want more to eat?' she asked, speaking slowly and distinctly.

'Grazie,' he said, 'Thank you,' and after taking a bite he continued falteringly, 'I speak little English. I come …' He hesitated. '… big boat, I run, bad man, I run, bad boys take money, take all.'

'Bad men, bad boys … he seems to have met a lot of bad people,' said Rhys, giving into hunger and opening his bag to rummage for his packed lunch.

'But you good. You help me.' The boy looked admiringly at Megan.

'Help *you*?' exclaimed Rhys. 'It's us who need help!'

'Let's sit down and eat. Then we can decide what to do,' said Megan. Rhys still kept a suspicious eye on Luigi but he had to admit to himself that the boy did not look as if he was much of a threat. He seemed to be slightly younger than them but he was considerably shorter and thinner and his dirty face bore the tracks of tears.

Rhys crammed a sandwich into his mouth. It had a reassuringly familiar taste in such strange surroundings. 'Oh, good, peanut butter,' he mumbled through a mouth full of bread.

He looked up and saw the longing look in Luigi's eyes. He offered him one of his sandwiches and Luigi accepted it gratefully, saying, 'Thank you. You good boy.'

'We had better keep some of our food for later,' said Megan, 'We don't know when we'll get any more.'

'We'll be back in the museum pretty soon though, Meg, won't we?' Rhys said hopefully.

'I don't know. We don't even know how we can get back or what we are here for.' Despite the worry she felt, she managed a reassuring smile. 'But we'll sort something out, I'm sure.'

She noticed that Luigi was staring at their clothes. They were both wearing their school uniform – black trousers, white t–shirts and red sweatshirts with the school crest discreetly embroidered on the front.

'Oh dear,' she said, 'I think we must look really strange to him.' Luigi was dressed in faded trousers which seemed to be too short for him and were streaked with dirt. He wore a rough jacket and had a battered pair of boots on his feet.

Megan exchanged a glance with Rhys. 'Perhaps we should take off our sweat shirts and put them in our bags. It's not too cold. And our trainers too. I don't think they had those in Victorian times.'

'Well, I'm not taking my trainers off,' declared Rhys. 'This ground is really rough.'

Megan sighed. Rhys could be so irritating, she thought. He didn't seem to understand that they needed to be safe. Rhys noticed her weary expression and said, more gently, 'So what do we do now?'

Megan spoke slowly. 'You know what I said about performing tasks like in a computer game … well, perhaps helping Luigi is one of the tasks.'

'That sounds nice and easy,' said Rhys sarcastically. 'We don't even know how to help him.'

'Don't you think it seems strange that Luigi is the first person we meet here? What was it that weird man in the museum said? Something about there being a lot of poor children who needed help.'

'Yes, but how do we actually get back to the museum?'

'Well, if the picture of the docks was a sort of bridge to the past perhaps we need to find another of the paintings that's in the museum now and try to go back through that.'

Luigi was frowning as he tried to understand what the children were saying.

'You help Luigi?' he said. He struggled to get something out of the inside of his jacket and Rhys leapt backwards, dragging Megan with him.

'Careful, Meg, he may be armed,' he declared, dramatically.

Chapter 6

LUIGI'S STORY

But the Italian boy had only pulled out a small folded piece of paper. He opened it and inside was a torn photo. He held it out to show them. It was faded and slightly blurred.

'My brother, Paolo' he said, pointing. Rhys and Megan moved closer and peered at the photo. The people in it looked stiffly posed and uncomfortable, like the ones in the old Victorian family photos that Megan's grandma had shown her. They recognized Luigi, although the boy in the photo was clean and neatly dressed; they could see too that the young man Luigi was pointing to had remarkably similar features to himself. There was an older woman sitting between them.

'Is that your mother?' Megan asked.

'Mama?' Luigi said. 'Si, she ...' He crossed himself and cast his eyes down.

'Has she died? Oh, I'm sorry,' said Megan and she reached out and stroked his arm sympathetically.

Luigi looked at her and a tear sparkled in the corner of his eye. 'You help me?' He was trying to smooth out the piece of crumpled paper that had been wrapped round the photograph. Bending over it, Megan could see some smudged and faded letters. It was still not light enough to make out the first two lines but the bottom line seemed to end in TOWN.

'Brother.' Luigi tapped the paper with his finger emphatically.

'Perhaps it's his brother's address but some of it is missing,' suggested Rhys, helpfully for once. The jagged edge of the paper showed that it had been torn at some point and it also looked as if it had come in contact with water.

Then he said something that sounded like 'meeseesproba.'

'Meeseeproba'? repeated Megan, blankly

'Si, meeseeproba.' He tapped the writing on the paper.

Megan and Rhys exchanged blank looks and repeated the word several times to get the sound of it. Suddenly Rhys said, 'Meesee – do you think that could be like Mrs?'

'All right,' replied Megan, considering the suggestion. 'So Mrs ... Proba? Proba? Does that make sense?'

'It sounds as if he's trying to say Mrs. Probert, like the dinner lady at school,' said Rhys.

'Si, si, lady – Mrs. Probert,' Luigi repeated excitedly.

'Perhaps that's the name of the lady whose house his brother is staying in,' said Megan.

'So all we have to do is find someone in Cardiff

called Mrs. Probert!' said Rhys. 'That should be easy-peasy – I don't think!'

'Oh, stop moaning!' snapped Megan, heaving her rucksack onto her shoulders, 'We're wasting time here – let's start looking.'

Chapter 7

THROUGH THE STREETS

The sun had come up now and was shining through a dusty haze as they set off again. They looked a strange, ill-assorted trio: Luigi a small, scruffy figure between his two taller, bulkier companions in their school uniform and with their brightly coloured bags on their backs.

Megan and Rhys could see now that they were in an area of warehouses and factories, looming brick buildings punctuated by tall chimney stacks. They crossed a bridge over a railway as a seemingly endless line of wagons loaded with coal rattled its way underneath. Ahead of them was a row of small, shabby houses. Some women were out sweeping their doorsteps and men in dull clothes and battered caps were setting off for work. There was a sour smell of drains and rotted food.

'We'll have to ask someone to help us but it would be better if we could get some different clothes to wear first. That woman's really staring at us.'

Rhys sighed. 'You're mad, Megs. We don't need different clothes, we need to go back to that place where the boats were, and then perhaps we'll find that we're in the museum again.'

'Well, I still think we need to help Luigi first. We can't just abandon him. We'll sort ourselves out later.'

Rhys' mouth drew into a cross, straight line. Megan continued, ignoring his sulky face. 'It's probably not a good idea to speak to a grown-up though because they'll ask us awkward questions. Perhaps we should ask someone our own age.'

They had come to a wider and busier street. Horse-drawn carts lumbered to and fro and smaller carriages with high-stepping horses darted amongst them. All across the skyline, they could see chimneys, belching out their smoke. A double-decker horse-drawn tram clattered past with a clanging of its bell.

'There are too many people here. Let's go down there,' Megan said, pointing to another side street lined with terraced houses. She could see some children ahead of them playing in the gutter. As they approached, the children turned from their game to stare at the three strangers. Their faces were thin and pinched–looking and their darting eyes were drawn to the bags that Megan and Rhys were carrying.

'They don't look very friendly,' muttered Rhys.

It was clear that Luigi was also feeling uneasy. He tugged at Megan's t-shirt.

'We go,' he said. 'They not good.'

They hastily crossed the street and hurried along to the corner. Two of the boys had stood up and started to follow them.

'Come on, I think we were safer in that busy street,' said Megan. They ran to the next turning and threaded their way through a maze of little streets that all looked the same until finally they found themselves back on the main thoroughfare.

They stopped on the corner and looked around. In one direction they could see cranes and the tall masts of ships reaching above the nearby roofs.

'That must be the way to Cardiff Bay' said Rhys, 'Let's go that way. That's where the Urdd hostel is where we're staying.'

'But it wasn't there in Victorian times, was it Rhys?' said Megan, with an exasperated sigh.

They had not noticed that while they were standing there, the two boys had caught up with them and suddenly, one of them made a grab for Rhys' bag while the other knocked Megan to the ground.

Chapter 8

THE TIME-MACHINE

Rhys staggered and almost fell but he was bigger and stronger than his assailant. He clung to his bag and kicked out with his trainers. Megan scrambled to her feet and Luigi, quick as a flash, hurled himself at the other boy like a small demon. Realizing that there was no contest, the two urchins let go of the bag and, dodging among the passers-by, disappeared from sight.

'Are you OK, Meg?' said Rhys, looking rather pale.

'Yes, I think so.' Megan rubbed her knees and Luigi patted her arm sympathetically.

'We need to hang onto our bags more tightly,' she said, shakily, 'and find some way of hiding them so that people don't stare at us so much.'

As they drew nearer to the masts and funnels they had seen earlier, the buildings became grander, with flights of steps leading up to large doors and imposing pillars along the front. Well-dressed men in dark suits were hurrying in and out or standing in groups absorbed in earnest discussions. They all wore tall hats and some had walking sticks or canes. It looked very different from the Bay area that Megan and Rhys had seen when they had arrived at the hostel, but through the hustle and bustle of carts and carriages and trams, the children spotted a familiar landmark: the red-brick clock tower of the Pier Head Building.

'Now we know where we are!' Rhys exclaimed.

Nearby, there was a landing stage where a steamer was tied up and passengers queuing to board. In the docks, to one side, large ships were moored and there was a constant rumble of loads of coal pouring down the shutes into their holds. Across the water of the bay, dotted with boats of all shapes and sizes, some with sails and some with smoking funnels, Megan recognized the headland of Penarth with the distinctive shape of St Augustine's Church tower which she knew from her visits to her grandparents. Not far away a small group of boys who looked to be about their age were leaning on the railings at the water's edge, chatting, laughing and eating.

'Perhaps we could ask one of those boys to help us,' said Megan. 'They look more friendly.'

One of them, a little apart from the others had a book open and was reading avidly while he stuffed some bread into his mouth. He looked up suddenly and stared in their direction. His eyes had a faraway look as if his mind was still half-buried in the story he had been reading.

'That one has a kind face,' Rhys said. The boy was the same height as Rhys and his clothes, although a little worn, were neat and clean. His eyes suddenly focused on them and he smiled.

'Hello,' he said, 'where have you come from? You look as if you're not from around here. Is this little urchin bothering you?'

'No, it's all right thanks. He's our friend,' said Rhys. 'We're trying to help him but actually we need a bit of help ourselves. He needs to find his brother but we don't really know where to look and it all looks so different …' His words came out in a garbled rush.

The boy was staring at their trainers and their back-packs.

'What are your names?' he asked. 'I'm Huw. Huw Morgan'

'I'm Megan and this is Rhys.'

'Megan? But that's a girl's name!' Puzzled, Huw glanced up and down at Megan in her school uniform.

'Yes, I am a girl actually.' Megan realized suddenly that the boy was surprised to see a girl dressed in trousers.

'Oh, so you are in disguise and have cut your hair!' he exclaimed. 'Have you and your brother run away from home?'

'He's not my brother, he's a friend from school,' said Megan.

The boy looked ever more puzzled.

'I would really like to hear your story,' he said, 'but I can't stay long because I have to go back to the office.'

'You work in an office?' Rhys said in surprise, 'but you look as if you're the same age as us.'

'Yes, I work in a shipping office over there. I'm twelve.'

'We're eleven,' said Megan. 'We're still at school.'

She had noticed the cover of the book that Huw was holding.

'What's your book called?' she asked.

Rhys sighed. 'Meg, you're such a geek sometimes. Why do you want to start talking about books now?'

Huw held it up for them to see.

'The Time Machine', he said, 'By Mr. Wells.'

'I thought so! Is it about someone who travels through time?' Meg recognized the title and thought that she had seen an old film of it once on television.

'Meg, what are you like? This is not an English lesson.'

'Do you know of it? It's very exciting. It's about a gentleman who builds a time machine and travels into the future'.

Megan took a deep breath and then said, rather breathlessly, 'Well, we seem to have done the same sort of thing, only we are from the future and we have travelled into the past. We live in the twenty-first century.'

Rhys groaned and shook his head. 'He's never going to believe that,' he said.

'By gosh, so you have travelled here in a time machine, exactly as in Mr. Wells' book!' exclaimed Huw.

'Only we don't exactly have a time machine and

we don't know what to do or how to get back home and we are frightened to ask anyone for help because they'll think that we're mad,' Megan said, relieved to be able to speak the truth to someone who seemed kind and trustworthy.

Huw was studying them with a slight frown on his face.

'Listen,' he said. 'I must hurry back to the office or I shall lose my position and then what would my mother do without my wages? I'll meet you here when I finish at five o'clock. You can see the time up there,' and he pointed to the large clock on the tower of the Pier Head Building.

'You do believe us, don't you?' Megan said pleadingly. 'We have nowhere to stay and we don't know our way around so we really do need some help. Oh, and we need to get some different clothes so that we fit in better.'

'Well, it is very difficult to believe what you have told me but, don't worry I'll try to help you. You seem like honest kids. I certainly can't take you home with me and explain such things to my mother, but my sister, Annie, has a friend whose mother runs a lodging house near here. You may be able to stay there. As for clothes, if you go straight up Bute Street you will see a big church, called St Mary's. It has two towers. You cannot miss it. The Sisters there give out clothes to the waifs and strays. I must go now. Don't forget, five o'clock just here. Then you can tell me everything.'

And with that, he stuffed the book in his pocket and, with a wave of his hand, set off at a run away from the dockside. Rhys and Luigi were watching him open-mouthed, but Megan, noticing the curious glances being cast in their direction, decided it would be best to move on.

'Come along,' she urged, 'the sooner we can get some more suitable clothes, the better.'

She took Luigi's hand and marched determinedly off in the direction the boy had pointed, with Rhys scurrying along behind.

Chapter 9

DRESSING THE PART

They soon spotted the silhouette of the church that Huw had described. There was a wall in front of it and a large, iron gate that was half open. A path led to the front porch and on either side there was a narrow strip of weedy grass, dotted with bushes and trees.

'Let's hide behind that bush and send Luigi in to get some clothes for us,' said Megan.

'But he can't speak English,' Rhys protested.

Megan opened her bag and fished out a rather battered note–book and a pencil. She tore out a page and wrote in capital letters, 'PLEASE I NEED CLOTHES FOR MY BROTHERS AND SISTERS'. Getting Luigi to understand what they wanted him to do took some time and a good deal of miming but, finally, he nodded vigorously although he was still rather reluctant to set off.

Just then, a little group of children, ragged and barefoot, trooped through the gate and walked round the side of the church towards a small door. It opened and the figure of an elderly woman in the black and white robes of a nun appeared, and ushered them in.

'She must be one of the Sisters Huw told us about. Go on Luigi.' Megan gave him a shove and indicated that he should follow them. Luigi seemed reassured by the sight of the nun. He nodded again and a smile lit up his face.

'I go,' he said. 'They good ladies. They in Italy also.'

'I hope he knows what to do,' muttered Rhys. 'We can't keep hiding all the time.'

They sat down on the grass then, realizing that they were both feeling tired and hungry after all their walking. Megan opened her back-pack.

'I've still got some biscuits somewhere,' she said. 'Shall we have one?'

While they were eating, the door opened again and Luigi came out carrying a bundle. He ran across the grass and joined them behind the bush. His face flushed with success, he handed the bundle to Megan with a flourish.

'Good?' he asked.

Megan opened it and the musty old-clothes smell that escaped made her wrinkle her nose. Seeing Luigi's look of disappointment, she hastened to reassure him.

'Very good, Luigi,' she said. 'Here, have a biscuit while I look at them.'

She pulled out a succession of unidentifiable garments. 'I'm sure we can find something here, can't we, Rhys?'

Rhys sniffed doubtfully but accepted the items she handed him. He reluctantly pulled on a pair of trousers in a coarse, scratchy material. They reached just below his knees and were tight round the waist. The bottoms of the legs were a little frayed. Once he had taken off his trainers and put on the pair of battered boots, he began to look the part.

'There's a jacket here as well,' Megan said. 'And a cap. You'd better have that. The other trousers look rather small and I'm not sure what these are but I think this skirt will fit me and I can put this old blanket or shawl or whatever it is round my shoulders over my t-shirt.'

'But there's only one pair of boots,' said Rhys, scrabbling through the clothes that were left.

Megan was struggling into the skirt. It came down almost to her ankles but was tight round the waist. She noticed that Luigi was staring at her, open-mouthed.

'You girl?' he asked, 'you not boy?'

Megan sighed.

'Yes, I'm a girl.' She smiled reassuringly.

'We'll never be able to explain everything to Luigi, will we,' she muttered to Rhys, while she slipped off her trainers and socks.

'Right,' she said, 'now that I look a bit more like the other poor children we've seen, I'll go back in there and see what else I can get.'

'You look too clean – and not thin enough,' said Rhys, with a grin.

'Well, I can't help that,' Megan said, giving him a playful shove, and ran off across the grass.

Chapter 10

MR. BARTHOLOMEW

Megan pushed open the side door of the church and found herself in a small, fusty-smelling room. The nun they had seen in the doorway and another younger nun were sorting through a pile of clothes on a trestle table. They looked up and smiled. Megan noticed that the younger nun was looking thoughtfully at her skirt and makeshift shawl.

'Please …,' Megan started, hesitantly. 'I wondered if you had any boots.'

She pointed to her bare feet which, now that they were exposed, looked very white and delicate, quite unlike the brown, hardened feet of the ragged children they had seen earlier. There was a tell-tale line where her socks usually ended and her legs above were tanned from wearing shorts.

'I will see what I can find for you.' The older nun did not seem to have recognized the clothes or noticed her white feet. Her younger colleague, however, was more curious.

'You are a very well-spoken young lady and you look very healthy. What lovely hair you have, although it is cut so short. Have you had a fever?'

Megan nodded uncertainly.

'And lovely white teeth,' the nun went on. 'What are you doing here begging for clothes?'

Before Megan could think of an answer, the door at the back of the room opened and an elderly man entered. He had a slight stoop and was dressed entirely in black except for his white dog-collar.

'Ah, Father Jones we have almost finished. We are just finding some boots for this young lady,' said the older nun. 'These look as if they might fit.'

Megan took them. 'Thank you very much,' she said, wondering how quickly she could leave and escape any more awkward questions.

'Try them on,' urged the man. 'You have time. I think that we have not seen you here before. We know most of the waifs and strays around this area.'

The younger nun said, 'She has a brother who does indeed look as if he is in need of our charity and seems to be unable to speak. Was it you who wrote the note for him to show us?'

'She seems to be quite an accomplished young lady,' the older nun chimed in.

'I must go now.' Megan said hurriedly, worried at the questioning. She felt that her face had turned bright red and that she must look extremely guilty. Catching sight of an old straw hat among the clothes on the table, she said, 'Please may I take the hat as well?' She thought that perhaps it would be better to hide her shiny clean hair.

'Thank you so much,' she said and made a dash

for the door. Before she could open it, Father Jones called after her, 'Come to Sunday School next week. And bring along your brothers and sisters.'

'Yes, yes, thank you…' she replied, becoming increasingly flustered as she struggled with the door catch.

At that moment, a voice called out from the other side of the church door, 'Are you in there, Father Jones? I need to speak to you.'

Megan froze – she had heard that voice before somewhere. She stepped back into the shadows. The door opened a crack and a face peeped round it.

It was the strange man from the museum.

He glanced quickly around the room and, as he turned to close the door behind him, his eyes met Megan's, just for a second. Did she imagine it – or did he seem to give her an almost invisible wink?

Megan was torn between the desire to speak to him and the need to get away from the inquisitive nun and priest as soon as possible. But they had turned towards the new arrival now, and seemed to have forgotten that she was there.

'Why, Mr. Bartholomew! We thought that you would not be here until tomorrow,' exclaimed the priest. 'The journey must have been very tiring in this warm weather. Sit down and Sister Angela will fetch you some water'.

Taking advantage of the moment's diversion, Megan managed at last to open the door and slip outside, closing it quietly behind her.

Chapter 11

A MISSED CHANCE?

Rhys was relieved to see Megan running back across the grass, some black boots in her hand and a battered straw hat rammed on her head.

'What's the matter Megan?' said Rhys, 'you look as if you've seen a ghost!'

'I've just seen Mr. Bartholomew,' gasped Megan.

'Who?'

'The strange man who spoke to us in the museum. Remember him? His name is Mr. Bartholomew. He came in to speak to the priest and the nuns and they seemed to know him.'

'That old weirdo who got us into this mess? Did you ask him how we could get back to the museum?'

'I didn't let on that I recognized him. He seemed to want me to go. It was as if he was helping me to get away from the priest and nuns because they were starting to ask me awkward questions about where I was from – but he winked at me. I know he did. It was definitely him.'

'Winked at you? You idiot, you should have spoken to him! He's our only help!'

'It's easy for you to say that. You haven't done anything to help since we left the museum, only moan and whine all the time,' Megan declared, angrily. She was beginning to wish that she had not run away so quickly. 'Wait here and look after our bags. I'm going to see if he's still there.' She glared at Rhys and flounced off across the grass.

Luigi glanced nervously after her then nudged Rhys gently.

'Why she angry?' he said, hesitantly. 'She not want help Luigi?'

Rhys sighed and managed a weak smile.

'No, Luigi, don't worry, she's not mad at you.'

He unfastened his back-pack and began rummaging around inside. Then he triumphantly pulled out a packet of crisps.

'I thought I still had some,' he said, ripping open the packet under Luigi's fascinated gaze. 'Let's share these while we wait. I'm starving.'

Luigi took one warily.

'Is good,' he announced, through a mouthful of crumbs.

They had just settled down to some serious munching when Megan came slowly back across the churchyard, her drooping shoulders and glum expression announcing before she arrived that she did not bring good news.

'Well?' Rhys asked tentatively.

'Gone, disappeared completely. I heard the young nun say that he had only come for a short visit and they didn't know when he would be back.'

'There's nothing we can do about it then. Come on, Meg, don't look so miserable – you're worrying Luigi. Have a crisp.'

Megan took one absent-mindedly. 'Oh well,' she said, 'perhaps we'll see him again somewhere – at least we know that he can travel through time like we did. I suppose we had better go back to the docks to meet Huw. Let's hope that he can help us.'

She picked up her back-pack with a sigh, but Luigi shook his head. 'Not good,' he said, 'bad boys see.'

'Luigi's right, we fit in better in these clothes, but our bags don't. Perhaps we could hide them in some of those old clothes that we haven't put on.' They managed to wrap their backpacks in a couple of the spare garments and tie up the bundles.

'Well done, Luigi, that was a good idea,' Megan said and Luigi beamed with satisfaction. Dressed in their assortment of ill-fitting clothes and with their back-packs now disguised as scruffy bundles, Megan and Rhys felt less conspicuous.

'You help me find brother?' Luigi asked, hopefully.

'Yes,' Megan, 'we help you find brother – but I'm afraid I have no idea where we are going to start.'

Chapter 12

OVER THE WALL

They reached the Pier Head Building as the clock on the tower said a quarter to five. Sitting down on a stone bench, they waited for Huw and watched the busy scene around them.

For a while, nobody said a word. The turmoil and the drama of the day was catching up with them a little, and each one was locked into a bubble of their own worries and longings.

Luigi looked again at his precious photo. Rhys thought of home, of a good plateful of hot food, and of his computer. Megan recalled wistfully her comfortable bedroom, with her cat curled up on the duvet among the scattered books and clothes. She tried to quell the rising sense of panic she felt inside.

Their thoughts were interrupted by the clock striking five o'clock and the clatter of boots running towards them.

'There you are! I thought you might not come back or that I had imagined you.' Huw had suddenly appeared at their side. 'You look much better like that. Oh – this is very exciting! I am looking forward enormously to hearing more about your time machine and what life is like in the future. But come along. I must not be too late arriving home or mother will fret. Let's go and find Annie.'

His lively energy cheered their flagging spirits, and they followed him away from the water front. He pointed out a two storey stone building nearby as they passed.

'That's the Pilotage Office,' he said, proudly. 'My father worked on the pilot boats that guide the big ships into the docks. It is very skilled work and well-paid. But since he died, we do not have so much money even though I work. My mother has to take in sewing to help make ends meet.'

'Oh, how sad!'

Memories of her own family flashed into Megan's mind and she suddenly felt very far away from them. She gave Huw a sympathetic look, and he smiled back.

'I live along here,' he said, as they came to a terrace of neat, well-kept houses opposite the stone seawall. 'I expect that my sister and her friend are playing on the mudflats over the wall.'

They could hear the murmur of children's voices with occasional high-pitched shrieks and bursts of laughter.

'Mother doesn't like Annie playing with Molly because ... well, she doesn't come from a very respectable family. Her mam's often not in the house and her father's away and her younger brother, Joe, runs wild. But Molly is good-hearted and tries to keep all her brothers and sisters in order.'

'Annie,' he called, then, he said in a low voice to Megan and Rhys, 'Best not to say anything about the time-travel matter. Just let me do the talking and go along with everything I say.'

'Annie, I have someone for you to meet,' he called. There was a scrabbling sound behind the wall and almost immediately a small, grinning face peeped over the top.

'Huw! You're home! Oh – who are those kids with you? Wait a mo …' There was some more scrabbling and whispering then the figure of a small girl appeared on top of the wall. She sat with her bare, muddy legs dangling over the edge and then slid expertly to the ground, smoothing down her skirt as she landed.

Behind her, other small faces popped up and a tall, gangly girl with a mass of tangled reddish curls appeared and jumped down. Her skirt was hitched up to reveal her muddy, grazed knees.

'Annie, I need to talk to you and Molly – without these little ones listening. It's a secret.'

'Ooh, a mystery,' exclaimed Molly, 'I love a mystery. Joe, you take Maire and Siobhan on home. This is important.'

Joe was a small, wiry boy with a dirty face and the same shock of red hair as his sisters. He scowled and muttered something under his breath but when Molly raised her arm, threateningly, he grabbed the younger children by the hand and dragged them away.

'I need to swear you to secrecy,' Huw said, when

50

they'd gone. 'These children need help. They have to keep away from grown-ups for a while and I thought perhaps you could take them back to your place, Molly – your mother probably won't even notice some extra kids in the house. I can give you some money for their keep.' He pulled some coins out of his trouser pocket and dropped them in her grubby hand. Megan felt a twinge of guilt when she remembered what Huw had told them about his family.

Molly jingled the coins and grinned at Megan, Rhys and Luigi.

'Sure, I can do that,' she said, 'Those two look like good kids. Come from a swanky home do they? Have they run away? The littl'un looks scared stiff, though. What's the matter with him?'

'He's Italian, stowed away on a boat and now he's been set upon and robbed. He's looking for his brother.'

'And where do the other two come from?' Annie was staring at them in fascination.

'Their names are Megan and Rhys,' said Huw. 'I can't tell you more at the moment, but they are helping Luigi.'

'Well, wherever you come from, we need to get back to my house or the others will have eaten all the supper, if there is any. Come along, it's not far.'

'Thank you, Molly, I knew you'd help. I'll come to see you tomorrow morning on the way to work. Bye.'

Molly was already chivvying them along the

street. She put her arm through Megan's in a friendly fashion and took Luigi's hand. She was obviously used to looking after younger children.

'It's very kind of you to help us, especially as you don't know us' said Megan. 'Won't your parents mind if you bring three extra children for a sleep-over?'

Molly giggled, 'I ain't heard that word before,' she said, 'There's only me Ma at home, Da's away. He's been away ages. Don't expect he's coming back. What with the lodgers and all, Ma's got her hands full. As long as I do me chores and look after the littl'uns and keep out of her hair, she'll be sweet.'

They came to a row of tall houses with peeling paintwork on the doors and windows. The glass panes were filthy and there were no curtains to speak of. Joe and the two little girls were sitting on the steps leading up to one of the doors.

'This is it,' said Molly cheerfully. 'Come on up.'

Megan and Rhys followed her into the dingy hall-way. Rhys tugged at Megan's sleeve and whispered,

'We can't just stay the night here with these children – we've only just met them and it all looks a bit, well, dirty. I don't like it here, Megs. Let's make a run for it.'

'Shush,' hissed Megan, 'What else can we do? It'll be better than spending the night out on the streets.' But as she followed Molly down the dark corridor and through a door into the kitchen, her heart sank.

What had they got themselves into?

Chapter 13

THE LODGING HOUSE

A large black pan was bubbling on the stove. Molly gave it a quick stir as she passed and yelled, 'Ma, we're home. Shall I give the kids their supper?'

A woman appeared in the doorway leading to the yard. Her face was flushed and she was balancing a baby on her hip. Before she could speak, Molly said hastily, 'Huw Morgan asked if we could let these three stay with us for the night. He's given me some money for their food. They're good kids.'

'I'm sure they are if Huw says so. He's a proper little gentleman. But I hope you've told them that it'll be a bit rough and ready here.'

'Thank you very much, Mrs…' Megan realized that she had no idea what Molly's surname was.

'O'Sullivan,' Molly said, taking the baby from her mother and jiggling it up and down when it started to cry. 'Me Mam's family came over from Ireland at the time of the famine.' With her other hand she was distributing an assortment of cracked and chipped bowls around the rickety-looking table in the centre of the room

'Sit down you two,' she said to Megan and Rhys.

'There's not enough chairs for all of us but the littl'uns usually sit on the step.'

Mrs.O'Sullivan was ladling some watery-looking broth into the bowls. Molly handed the baby over to the bigger of her two little sisters, who seemed to be called Maire, and began cutting slices off a large loaf of bread.

Although there was very little meat in the soup and the vegetables were sparse as well, it was hot and made the stale bread easier to chew. Megan and Rhys ate with relish, mopping up their bowls in the same way as the O'Sullivan children. Mrs. O'Sullivan was sitting in the corner, a glass of ale in her hand, and showed no further interest in the children, now that Molly was home to do the work.

With their bellies full of warmth, and surrounded by chatter and kindness, all of a sudden a wave of tiredness crept over Megan and she yawned widely. It was catching – Rhys found himself doing the same.

'Are you tired?' asked Maire. 'Have you come a long way today?'

'Yes, a very long way,' said Megan, finding it hard to remember how and where the day had started. It all seemed like a dream – but the chipped bowls, the sour smell of the dirty kitchen and the touch of Maire's small sticky hand on her arm were all real enough. She felt suddenly that all she wanted to do was lay down somewhere and go to sleep. Perhaps in the morning everything would make sense.

'I'll show you where you can all sleep,' Molly said. 'You look as if you need it. And you,' she added, putting an arm round Luigi's shoulders, 'sure, you have the most beautiful dark eyes. You'll break some poor girl's heart one day.'

Luigi looked puzzled but, reassured by the warmth in her words he smiled shyly at her as she led them up the stairs.

'The privy's across the yard and there's water in the scullery – and more in the pump outside if you need it,' Molly went on. Megan and Rhys stumbled along behind her, too sleepy to take in much of what she was saying. It briefly crossed Megan's mind that she did not have her toothbrush and flannel with her but they were now rather vague objects from a different world when she tried to focus on them.

Molly opened the door to a cramped attic room with sloping walls and two small rickety-looking beds.

'You two boys will have to squeeze in with Joe,' she said. 'And Megan, you'll be in with us.'

Megan was relieved to see that the children did not have night clothes. They just took off their dresses and trousers revealing grubby under garments which looked like long-johns and vests. Megan and Rhys managed as best they could – they had only acquired a top layer of Victorian clothes from the nuns at St Mary's. Rhys looked despairingly at Megan then decided to keep his trousers on. She had already slid under the blanket, too tired to worry about explanations.

'Goodnight,' she said, yawning again.

'You haven't said your prayers.' Maire was kneeling beside the bed with little Siobhan at her side.

'Leave her,' Molly said, 'I'm sure the Lord will understand.'

The bed was lumpy and the pillow hard but as soon as Megan lay down and closed her eyes, she began to drift off to sleep, lulled by the murmur of voices as the children recited their prayers.

Chapter 14

THE SEARCH BEGINS

Megan woke slowly in the hazy morning light to find herself caught in a tangle of limbs and bedclothes, a small elbow digging in her side. A tiny voice was saying 'Wake up, wake up,' and she felt small grubby hands stroking her face. She opened her eyes to see little Siobhan staring at her with her large dark eyes.

'She's awake, Molly,' she shouted.

'Come on you sleepy-head, Huw and Annie will be here in no time,' said Molly, with a grin. 'The boys are already up.'

Megan yawned, stretched, and looked at the grubby bed-covers scattered around her. There was a strong smell of unwashed bodies and stale air.

In the kitchen, Rhys and Luigi were tucking into a chunk of bread.

'Megan!' Rhys exclaimed 'You took your time! They don't seem to bother much about washing or having a shower here – it's really cool.'

'That's because they don't have a bathroom,' Megan said, in a whisper, 'Be careful what you're saying. It's kind of them to let us stay here when they are so poor.'

The bread was hard and there was nothing to put on it but Megan was hungry and ate it greedily. She was in the unfamiliar position of having no idea where her next meal would be coming from, so any food was gratefully received.

Molly dashed into the kitchen.

'Huw and Annie are here,' she said. 'Joe, you keep an eye on these little'uns while I go to talk to my friends.'

Huw and Annie were standing outside in the yard.

'I hope that we didn't wake you too early,' Huw said, 'but I have to go to work and we need to talk first. Annie can come with you this morning to look for Luigi's brother.' Annie grinned and winked at Megan.

'Don't you have to go to school?' Megan asked.

'But it's the holidays – aren't you on holiday too?' Molly said.

'Yes, of course,' Megan said, hastily, covering up her mistake. 'Now, where's that paper with your brother's address, Luigi?'

'Ah, si...' Luigi pulled the increasingly scruffy scrap of paper from his pocket and tried to smooth out the creases.

The first line of writing had disappeared almost entirely and they could only make out a B and a T. Underneath, there was an I, a D and an E printed, and then STREET. The last line said TOWN.

'And Luigi also kept saying something that sounded like 'Mrs. Probert',' said Rhys.

'Well, there's a Mrs. Probert who runs a lodging house in Adelaide Street – number 44, I think,' said Molly, eagerly. 'She's a snooty old cow – had a run-in with my Ma once. Said my Ma ran a disreputable place and gave respectable landladies like her a bad name.'

'Yes, that looks as if it could be Adelaide Street and the last line must be Butetown,' said Huw, studying the paper closely.

'I know where Adelaide Street is!' volunteered Annie, 'I'll take you there, but I have to be back at home by noon.'

'I'd come with you too but I have to mind the kids, worst luck,' said Molly with a sigh.

'I can come and take care of Rhys and Megan all day, and make sure they come to no harm.' Joe had crept out of the house and was trying to see what they were all looking at. Huw seemed doubtful.

'Well, I'm not sure …' He knew that Joe was always getting into mischief.

Molly gave her brother a sharp smack around the head that made Rhys wince in sympathy.

'I told you to stay inside,' she said.

'But I know all the streets round here like the back of my hand. Rhys and his sister will come to no harm if they're with me.'

'Megan's not my …' Rhys started and then, seeing Megan's frown, he stopped.

'He might be useful,' Megan said, remembering the hostile children they had run into the previous day.

Joe beamed at her.

'Well, these kids are toffs, Joe,' said Molly. 'You need to look after them, and if I find out that you've gone off with any of those street urchins you hang around with, there'll be no supper for you all week, I swear.'

They arranged to meet Huw at the Pier Head when he finished work, but before he left, he took Megan and Rhys aside and said, quietly, 'I thought it best to tell Annie where you have come from but I wouldn't let on to anyone else, if I were you.'

Then they set off, Annie linking her arm through Megan's and the boys walking behind, chatting happily.

'Huw told me that you have travelled here from the future by some sort of magic,' whispered Annie. 'I thought that he'd spent too much time with his nose stuck in that book of his and that he'd gone soft in the head, but Huw doesn't usually make things up. Anyhow, wherever you're from, this is fun! A mysterious quest to find a missing person, just like in the newspapers.'

Megan smiled at her. It was nice to have a friend in this strange new place, so different from her own world at home.

She thought about the O'Sullivan family as they

strolled along. She had noticed how Molly looked no older than she was and yet she had to take care of Maire and little Siobhan and keep Joe from getting into scrapes. To Megan that was an appalling prospect.

'Does Molly have to look after her sisters very often?' she asked Annie.

'Most of the time, in the school holidays. She cares for the baby too sometimes and her Mam often keeps her off school as well so poor Molly gets in trouble with her teachers and falls behind in her learning.' said Annie.

'Those teachers are miserable, dried-up old sticks, anyway,' said Joe, who was listening to their conversation. 'Who wants to be shut up in a dreary classroom doing sums that make no sense?'

'Joe doesn't go to school very often,' said Annie, disapprovingly.

'I'm not such a fool as you are, Miss Prim-and-Proper,' Joe said, sticking his tongue out at Annie.

'So what do you do all day?' Rhys asked, a look of admiration on his face.

'I go off and make myself a bit of money, that's what. After all, Ma's never got any and you've seen what it's like in the house. There are lots of kids who live on the streets in Cardiff 'cos they're orphans or have run away from home. And there are lots of people who have plenty of money, if you see what I mean'

'You mean you *steal*?'

'Well, perhaps a bit of 'borrowing' here and there, as we say – some of them folks deserve to have their pockets picked. But there are good folks too who give out clothes and food to the waifs and strays. There was a grand tea for them all a few weeks back when it was the Jubilee of the old Queen. I ate so much I thought I'd burst.'

'Stop your showing off Joe, I think we're there. You keep well back and let me do the talking,' said Annie.

She climbed the steps and knocked on the front door.

They had arrived at 44, Adelaide Street, Butetown.

Chapter 15

NOT WELCOME!

Nothing happened for what seemed like an age and then the door opened slightly and the pale face of a young girl peeped out.

'What do you want?' she said, scowling at them.

'Can we speak to Mrs. Probert, please?' asked Annie.

'You're not begging, are you?'

'Who is it, Minnie?' called a voice from down the hallway.

'Some kids want to speak to you, Mrs. Probert.'

'Children? What do they want?'

A middle-aged woman with a careworn face and her hair pulled back into a tight, unflattering bun came to the door and cast a rapid glance over the little group.

Megan stepped forward.

'Please, Mrs. Probert,' she said, 'we are looking for a boy, well, a man, called Paolo who came here from Italy. We think he's staying here with you and Luigi here is his brother and is looking for him. He has your address and a photograph of him.'

The woman had stiffened when she heard the name and put her hand up to her face.

'Is here? Paolo is here?' said Luigi, running up the steps.

The woman gave a gasp, seeing the likeness between the two brothers, 'Well, I...I...' she stammered. 'Oh – you look so ...'

'What is it, Ada? Is there some trouble?'

A pompous voice interrupted her thoughts, then the door was flung back and a man appeared. He wore a shabby black jacket buttoned tightly across his bulging stomach. His eyes were cold and hostile.

'They are asking for Paolo ...'

'Paolo? That thief! Tell them to get off my doorstep at once or ...'

'This boy says he's Paolo's brother.'

'So he's a thief too I expect!' He took a threatening step towards Luigi and loomed over him, his stomach wobbling with rage.

'Well, you're not going to get into my house. If I don't see the back of you this instant, I'll call the police!'

Luigi's expression had turned from one of eager anticipation to one of terror and confusion.

'What he say? Where my brother?' he stammered.

The man raised his arm to strike him but Annie stepped between them and pulled Luigi away by his arm.

'He hasn't done anything,' she said, 'He just wanted to find out where his brother is. He has no other family here.'

'Well, I'd like to know where his brother is too and so would Mrs. Probert, whose jewellery he stole. I know where he should be – behind bars! But he's disappeared off the face of the earth, hasn't he? No sign of him, even though the police have been looking for him all around the Docks. Probably found himself a ship and is back in Italy now laughing at us all. Now get out of my sight or I'll make sure that snivelling little wastrel is locked up instead.'

Luigi, still not understanding what had happened but certain that it was something bad, had started to sob pathetically. Megan put her arm round him and drew him away from the furious man. A little crowd of people had gathered on the opposite side of the street and were watching the confrontation with interest.

'Come on,' Annie said, nervously, 'No point in hanging around here.'

Joe looked as if he wanted to stay and argue with Mr. Probert but Annie grabbed his arm and set off at a run. Rhys and Megan followed, dragging the sobbing Luigi along with them.

For a little while, they had seemed to be so close to success …

Chapter 16

A CHANGE OF FORTUNE

When they had turned into the next street, Annie stopped by the window of the grocer's shop on the corner so that they could all get their breath. Megan peeped warily back round the corner to check that no-one was following them. A crowd of bystanders was still gathered there, and she could see Mr. Probert waving his arms about excitedly.

She managed to explain to Luigi what Mr. Probert had said and Luigi was sobbing more than ever and repeating, 'No, not true. Paolo not bad. He good boy.' In his hand he was still clutching his torn photo. They stood in a dejected little huddle, calming him down and comforting him as best they could.

Then, all of a sudden –

'Ah, you're still here! I hoped I'd catch you!' The voice of Mrs. Probert startled them all and they spun round to see her standing there, clutching a woollen shawl round her shoulders and glancing nervously behind her from time to time.

'We're just on our way,' said Megan, grabbing Luigi's hand and starting to walk away.

'No, wait,' the woman said. She looked at Luigi who was rubbing at his tear-stained face with his grubby hands, and her lips twitched slightly as if she was trying to hold back tears herself.

'Such a handsome boy, he was. I just don't understand how he could …' Her voice trailed away.

'Look, I've brought you these,' she went on, and thrust a plain brown envelope into Luigi's hands.

She turned to the others.

'When his brother disappeared,' she said, 'I found these left behind in his room. I kept them in case he returned. Don't breathe a word to my husband, will you?' She looked behind her warily as she spoke.

Luigi had opened the envelope eagerly. Inside was a small photo that looked as if it had been taken recently. The cardboard mount was crisp and unstained and the gold lettering with the name of the photographic studio was still bright – 'T.L. Howe. 41, Windsor Road, Penarth.'

'Paolo!' exclaimed Luigi. The others crowded round to look at the picture. It was of a young couple, posing in front of a balustrade festooned with flowers. The young man was the one in Luigi's tattered photo but, instead of standing stiffly with a serious expression, he was smiling confidently, one arm resting on the shoulders of a pretty girl in a beribboned straw hat who was seated at his side. Together with the photo there was a newspaper cutting that Luigi unfolded and handed to Megan with a puzzled look on his face.

'It's about Mr. Marconi's experiments with the

telegraphy,' explained Mrs. Probert, 'He cut it out of the newspaper – really excited he was, about this Mr. Marconi, said that Italy would be proud of him and that this telegraphy fandango would transform the world. That was why he went to Penarth – to see the place where Mr. Marconi made his experiment, and that's where he met the girl, Sarah I think her name was.'

Her words came out in a rush.

'He was very sweet on her, showed me the photo and said that he was hoping to get married to her as soon as he had enough money to make sure that his family in Italy was well taken care of. He seemed such a good boy.'

She sighed and then took a quick look round the corner towards her house.

'I'd best be getting back,' she said anxiously, 'before Mr. Probert returns.'

'And then Paolo just disappeared?' asked Megan.

'Well, he seemed to change – he wasn't so cheerful any more. He seemed troubled and he stopped chatting to me when he got back from the docks. And often he didn't come home till late and I'd swear that there was the smell of drink on him sometimes. But still, just to disappear like that and to take my necklace … It just goes to show that you can't trust no-one. Anyway, you can keep those. Your little friend seems to like the picture,' and she looked at Luigi with an expression that was almost tender.

'So like him, he is. Let's hope he doesn't turn out the same.' She gathered her shawl around her again and seemed ready to leave, then had second thoughts and thrust her hand in her pocket.

'Here,' she said, handing Megan some coins, 'get some sweets for yourselves. Your brother will fair wear out that window by staring at it so.' Rhys had turned to look longingly at the tempting array of sweet jars in the shop window while the woman had been talking.

Megan looked at the coins in her hand with surprise.

'Oh, thank you,' she said. 'You're very kind.' Mrs. Probert gave a half grimace that was almost a smile and after one more quick glance at Luigi, turned and hurried back along the street towards her house.

'Well,' said Annie, 'So she's not such a miserable old sour puss as we thought. Come on, let's go into the shop!'

Chapter 17

MORE INFORMATION

The jangle of the door-bell announced their entry into the shop, although the shop-keeper, a stout, bald-headed man in a brown apron, did not need to be alerted, as he had been peeping through the merchandise in his window to keep an eye on what was happening outside.

'Well, it's your lucky day with no mistake,' he exclaimed, 'or else my eyes were deceiving me! Did I see Ada Probert give some money to children?'

'Yes, and we'd like to buy some sweets please. Do you know Mrs. Probert?' inquired Megan.

'I know everyone around here,' said the man, taking some paper from a spike on the counter and twisting it into cones. 'She has a reputation for being a bit of a sour old stick but I'm not surprised really with a husband like hers. Now let's see how much you've got and what you'd like to buy.'

The boys were already studying the contents of the colourful jars eagerly, but Megan had another idea. Shopkeepers always know the people who live in an area, she thought. She'd give it a try.

'We're looking for Luigi's brother, Paolo, who used to lodge at Mrs. Probert's. Did you know him?' she asked.

The shop-keeper looked curiously at Luigi.

'I thought he reminded me of someone,' he said. 'Yes, I knew him – he often used to come in here, a nice, friendly cheerful chap at first.' He hesitated.

'What happened to him?' asked Megan.

'He got in with a bad crowd down at the 'Packet'. I know that Mr. Probert says as he stole some of his wife's jewellery before he disappeared but I reckon that Harry Jenkins has got a lot to answer for.' He shook his head knowingly.

'Who's Harry Jenkins?' asked Annie.

'You don't want to get mixed up with him. He's a nasty piece of work. Oh, he seems nice enough – cheerful, friendly, life-and-soul-of-the-party sort of chap. But looks can deceive. That was the trouble. The Italian boy was lonely, missing his home and family and Harry comes along and makes friends with him. He seemed to change then, this Paolo, not so talkative when he came in – looked worried, even smelt of the drink at times. I tried to warn him about Harry, but he was having none of it. Then he stopped coming in altogether and soon after, I heard that he'd scarpered. Anyway, I need to get on with my work. Hurry up and choose your sweets. They'll cheer the little one up a bit.'

When they had paid, Mr. Pritchard put his hand into a large tin on the counter and took out a handful of biscuits that he put into a brown paper bag, twisting it at the corners, and handing it to Megan.

'There's something in there to keep you all going. And be careful – best not to get mixed up in anything that Harry Jenkins has a hand in!'

It was clear that Joe was bursting to say something but he held his tongue until they were outside. Then, he said, triumphantly,

'I told Molly that I could be of help to you in your search but she never takes any notice of what I say. Listen.' He paused dramatically, then declared, 'I know this Harry Jenkins, 'cos he hangs out in the pub where a mate of mine lives – he's a wrong'un and no mistake. I might be able to find out a bit more about what went on. You respectable kids can't be going to the sort of places where Harry goes, but nobody would turn a hair if I was seen there.'

'Well, you had better come to our meeting with Huw later, if you swear that you won't tell anyone else about us,' Megan said. 'We are going to need all the help we can get!'

'I have to go back home now or Mam will be anxious,' said Annie, 'so remember what Molly said, Joe – you're not to get into any trouble and you are to be at the Pier Head with Megan and Rhys at five o'clock.'

'Don't you worry,' said Joe, breezily, 'I'll look after them as if they were the old Queen herself.'

Chapter 18

LOOKING FOR THE MUSEUM

'Where are we going, Joe?' said Megan, as he set off with them in a purposeful fashion towards the centre of the city.

'I've got a bit of business to do at the station first,' he said, with a mischievous grin. 'Begging not thieving,' he hastened to add, seeing Megan's look of concern, 'and perhaps we might even get something tasty to eat afterwards.'

The streets near the station were busy and noisy. Travellers were alighting from carriages and trams and porters were hauling cases and trunks, while street sellers loudly proclaimed their wares and ragged children dodged among the crowds.

'This looks promising,' said Joe, with a grin. 'Give me your cap, Rhys.'

Megan noticed that there were a number of urchins outside the station, huddled together with outstretched hands or rattling battered tin cups for change.

Joe led the way into the station's grand entrance hall.

'Hold the cap out, Luigi,' he muttered, 'there's a

group of young ladies coming who look like a soft touch.'

He shoved Luigi in front of them and called out, 'Please, spare a penny for the sake of me brother. We're orphans and he's poorly and I've got no money for medicine. Please lovely ladies. I'm sure that you have kind hearts.'

'Oh, what a sweet child,' one of them exclaimed, staring at Luigi, 'such beautiful eyes and he looks so sad.'

She stopped to look for a coin in her purse and dropped it into the cap, but her friend dragged her away, saying, 'Do come on, Cecily, you should not encourage them. There are Societies that look after orphans these days.'

However, a motherly-looking woman, poorly dressed but with a kindly face, dropped a small coin into the outstretched cap.

'God bless you, boy,' she said as she passed, and Luigi responded with a charming smile. Joe looked on approvingly.

'Good work,' he said, with satisfaction, 'but we had better scarper. I can see a rozzer coming.'

A policeman was strolling through the crowd scanning the people he passed. Before he reached them, however, Joe had hustled them all towards a side entrance. Once outside, he stopped and inspected the contents of the cap.

'Not bad,' he said, 'Luigi's dark eyes and sad face

will make us a bit more money yet and we'll soon have enough for a nice hot pie.' A group of sharp-eyed urchins were eying them curiously.

'Hey, Joe, who're your friends?' one of them called.

'None of your business,' he shouted back.

He steered them quickly along the alley way to the station forecourt.

'Come on, let's get out of here. We don't want those kids nicking our takings'.

'Is the Castle near here?' Megan asked as they walked briskly through the crowds. If this was the centre of Cardiff, it looked very different from the city she remembered from her visits with her grandparents.

'Yes. Why? Are you thinking of calling on his Lordship?' Joe sniggered.

'There's a building we want to find, that's all,' said Megan.

'It's this way,' replied Joe ahead of them, veering slightly to the left. 'Come on.'

'You mean the Museum, Megs?' whispered Rhys.

She nodded.

Rhys looked pleased. Was this the moment they might be able to sneak away and return home? he wondered. He was excited at the thought that this strange adventure might be nearly over; that they could soon be back safely with the rest of their class.

As they walked on, Megan realized that, although the people and the vehicles all looked strange, there was something familiar about the street they were in and she began to feel that it would be easy to find their way to the Museum. Rhys had also recognized the street.

'This is the way to the Castle!' he said to Megan.

'There's your Castle,' said Joe, echoing his words.'What now?'

Megan and Rhys looked where Joe was pointing. 'Well, I can see the Clock Tower's there,' said Megan, slowly, 'and the wall with the animals on top – but it looks really different with all those old houses in front of it. Can we go along there, down the other side of the Castle, by the wall?'

'There isn't much along there,' said Joe dismissively, 'just some old ruins and the big park where Lord Bute grazes his cattle.'

'But what about the City Hall and the Museum?' asked Megan, thinking of the elegant white stone buildings which made up the centre of her capital city, and the tower of the City Hall with its golden clock.

Joe shrugged his shoulders.

'Don't know what you mean,' he said, 'You kids ask some strange questions.'

As they seemed reluctant to accept his word for it and turn back, Joe sighed and went on, 'If you don't believe me, I'll show you. Come on.'

He strode ahead while Megan and Rhys looked around them. Apart from the castle walls, there was nothing that they remembered from present day Cardiff. There was no City Hall, no Museum, no fountain, no neat flowerbeds. Just the ornamental gates of a park, with grass and trees stretching into the distance.

Rhys and Megan looked at each other. Surely there was some mistake?

Because if there was no Museum ... how would they ever be able to return home?

Chapter 19

ANOTHER PLAN

Megan and Rhys stood and stared in dismay. Joe looked triumphant.

'No point in going any further,' he said. Then, suspiciously, 'So, if you're not from around here, where have you come from? Have you run away from home?'

'Yes, that's right,' said Megan. They wouldn't be returning home in a hurry, she thought sadly. So she had better make sure they had a good story to tell people. After all, Luigi and Huw had both thought that they were runaways. Remembering fairytales she had read, she said, 'We've run away from our wicked step–mother and we are in disguise.' She looked at Rhys and raised her eyebrow.

'Yes,' said Rhys, approvingly, and changed the subject. 'Now didn't you say something about getting a pie, Joe?'

They wandered slowly back towards the docks, stopping off on Queen Street to buy a steaming hot meat pie with Luigi's earnings from that morning. The day had not turned out as Megan and Rhys had hoped. They hadn't found Luigi's brother and there seemed to be no way home. They would just have to be patient. What choice did they have?

When they arrived at the Pier Head they found that there was still some time left before Huw would be there, so they sat down on the edge of the dock to watch the comings and goings. The ferry to Penarth was about to leave and Megan remembered the photo and cutting that Mrs. Probert had given Luigi.

'Can I see that photo of your brother and his girlfriend?' she said.

Luigi took it out of the envelope with great care. They all peered at it.

'Looks quite the gent doesn't he?' said Joe.

'I was wondering if we could go to Penarth and find the girl. She might know where Paolo is.'

'But we don't know where she lives,' said Rhys.

'Well, the address of the photographer is on the photo. Perhaps we could go there and see if they know her,' Megan suggested.

'So there you are! What are you looking at?' a voice exclaimed, just behind them.

'Huw! Have you finished work already?'

'Yes, I managed to complete all my tasks really quickly so that my boss would let me leave early. I've been worrying about you all day.'

'Well, here they are, safe and sound,' said Joe.

'And we have a lot to tell you,' said Megan, 'and Joe has some useful information.'

They told him the whole story and showed him the photo and the newspaper cutting. He peered closely at them.

'Yes,' he said, 'I remember hearing about this Mr. Marconi and his telegraphy experiments. Tomorrow is Saturday so I only have to work in the morning. When I finish, we could take the ferry to Penarth. You can come too Joe, as you are helping us. I can pay for us all. And I think that it is a very good idea if you can find out something more about this Harry Jenkins before then.'

'Pleased to be of assistance,' said Joe, beaming, 'I'll get on to it right away. Tell Molly I'm off on some important business. See you tomorrow'

'Be careful, won't you Joe?' Megan put a restraining hand on his arm. 'Harry Jenkins may be dangerous and I wouldn't want you to get hurt.'

'Don't you worry. I can look after myself.'

After Joe had left them, Megan said, hesitantly,

'We need to talk to you about something else. Something really important' The disappointment of not finding the Museum had been gnawing away at Megan all afternoon and she desperately needed to share her thoughts with someone she could trust.

'Well, I'll walk back to Molly's with you.' replied Huw, with a worried look. 'Were you alright there last night? I know it's not very grand but at least Molly's mam asks no questions.'

They assured him that everyone had been very kind. Megan did not mention the itchiness that she had suffered all day and Rhys did not complain about the poor food.

'The thing is,' said Megan, 'we need to find out how to get back to our own century, you see.'

As they walked, they told Huw about their visit to the National Museum with their class, and about the painting and Mr. Bartholomew.

'But, we've just found out today that the Museum hasn't been built yet,' explained Megan, sadly.

'So your time machine was just a painting,' said Huw. He looked a little disappointed but then said, as if to convince himself, 'But the important thing is that you have actually travelled through time. So, perhaps we do not need to build complicated time machines. We just have to find the things in our own life that can act as time machines. But since you came here through a painting … well … that may be the way you can return. The only museum in Cardiff with paintings that I know of is in the Central Library. There are many interesting exhibits there – old rocks and stones and strange animals and things. And in a room at the top of the building there are some paintings and sculptures. It's in a street called The Hayes.'

'I know that building,' exclaimed Megan, 'it's still there, only now it's called The Old Library because there's a big new library further along the street. We could go tomorrow morning and have a look at the pictures – perhaps we'll find the painting that we need.'

And with that renewed hope, they hurried 'home'.

Chapter 20

THE MUSEUM

The sun was shining through the grimy window when they woke up the next morning. Joe, who had come in very late from making his 'enquiries', was still fast asleep so they decided not to wake him. They would go to the Cardiff museum by themselves and that way, they wouldn't have to answer his questions. Luigi seemed only too pleased to stay with Molly, helping to mind the little'uns.

As they turned into Bute Street, Rhys looked longingly at the horse-pulled trams that were passing.

'I wish we could go on one of those,' he said. 'I'm tired of this walk. It's a long way from the docks to the centre, Megs'

'Well, you can't because we don't have any money,' snapped Megan, secretly feeling the same.

They walked under the railway bridge and then down St Mary's Street and through the Royal Arcade into the Hayes.

'I remember this,' said Rhys, with satisfaction, 'It's where the Tourist Office is and that exhibition on the history of Cardiff!'

There was a man in a dark suit and peaked cap at the door to the museum.

'Where do you think you're going then?' he growled, eyeing them with suspicion.

'We've come to see the paintings in the art gallery,' said Megan with her sweetest smile.

'It's not open yet.'

'Oh no,' groaned Rhys, 'don't say we've walked all that way for nothing.'

'What's going on here, Dawkins?' said a voice nearby. An elderly man, carrying a leather bag was approaching the steps.

'These children say that they want to see the art gallery, sir. Up to some sort of mischief, no doubt. I've told them that it's closed.'

'We just wanted to look at the paintings, sir' said Megan.

'And we've walked a long way,' added Rhys.

The man inspected them thoughtfully.

'Well, I am very pleased to meet young people who are so eager to look at paintings. They can come up with me Dawkins. I'll keep an eye on them.'

The doorman sighed. 'Mind you behave yourselves then and don't go touching anything,' he warned, as he opened the door and stood back respectfully to let the elderly gentleman pass.

The children followed him along a brightly tiled corridor to the stairs.

'Now, are you ready for a climb?' he said, with a smile. 'There are seventy steps up to the museum and art gallery.'

At the top, he stopped to get his breath and then said,

'I'll open up the natural history room first. I'm sure that you will find the geological specimens and the stuffed birds of interest.'

The room he unlocked had long lines of glass-topped cases down the centre containing examples of different sorts of rocks, all neatly labelled. Around the walls there were larger cases housing a variety of stuffed birds. To Megan and Rhys it looked very fusty and boring compared with the museums that they had visited. No buttons to press. No interactive screens. They looked around dutifully.

'And now for the Art Gallery,' declared the elderly gentleman after a few minutes, seeing that Megan and Rhys were not really interested in the stuffed birds. They followed him into a smaller room with paintings hung around the walls.

'There,' he said, proudly. 'This is the Menelaus Room which now houses Cardiff's collection of paintings.'

'Is this it?' asked Rhys in amazement. The old gentleman looked rather disappointed at his tone.

'Yes,' he said, 'but I am sure that we shall be going from strength to strength. There are plans afoot to build a large new museum and art gallery like those that already exist in Birmingham and Liverpool. Perhaps you have visited one of those, if you find this inadequate.'

'I've been to the one in Birmingham,' said Megan, eager to please him, 'but this is very nice. We really wanted to look at the pictures here.'

Opposite them was a painting in tones of grey and pale blue of a rocky coast and the moonlight shining across the sea. 'I really like this one,' she continued.

'Ah, that is one of our newer purchases,' the old gentleman explained, beaming with pleasure. 'By Mr. Lionel Walden, an American gentleman who has painted several pictures of this area.'

'Wasn't that the name of the painter who...' Rhys started, and exchanged glances with Megan. She hushed him with a glare.

'Do you have any more by him?' asked Megan.

'No, only this one at present.'

'I don't remember any of these from the museum do you, Rhys?' whispered Megan. Rhys shook his head.

'And I don't feel that sort of pulling-us-in feeling that we had when we looked at the picture of the docks,' he whispered back.

'Perhaps that's because we haven't managed to find Luigi's brother yet,' said Megan. 'We haven't really helped anyone.'

So as not to disappoint the old gentleman, they looked at each of the other pictures in the room in turn, then Rhys asked quietly, 'Shouldn't we be going? I've no idea what the time is.'

Hearing him, the old gentleman pulled a gold

watch on a chain out of his waistcoat pocket and said, 'Oh dear, I must go too. I have an important meeting. Well – it is very gratifying to see such an interest in art in the young. I've no doubt that you will live to see the new art gallery and museum that is being planned – if ever it gets built. There have been so many meetings and discussions and arguments over the years – sometimes, I despair. Let us hope that the twentieth century will see some progress being made, eh? '

'Oh, I'm sure that it will be built,' said Megan, feeling a little sorry for him, 'and that it will be really good and lots of people will visit it.'

'Well, I wish I had your optimism young lady.' The old gentleman ushered them towards the stairs. 'Now you had best be on your way. Here, take these.' He rummaged in his pocket and pulled out two coins and gave one to each of them.

'You look as if you do not come from wealthy families although you are so well spoken. I hope to see you again one day.' And he raised his top hat and departed down the stone stairs, with a swish of his cane.

Megan and Rhys looked down at the two coins with delight.

'Well, this time we *can* ride on one of those trams,' Rhys declared, triumphantly, as they ran down the stairs. 'We have some money now!'

Chapter 21

FERRY TO PENARTH

The children squeezed onto a tram that was going to the Pier Head. Rhys was bubbling with excitement and insisted on going upstairs, but Megan felt a little apprehensive. The seats were hard and the vehicle seemed to sway alarmingly when it set off, but she had to admit that it was an exhilarating ride, out in the open air behind the two sweating horses, who were straining to pull their heavy load.

'That was really cool,' exclaimed Rhys, as they tumbled down the stairs, dishevelled and breathless, at the dockside.

It was a warm and sunny day, with just a few clouds building up inland. Groups of people were already beginning to queue for the next ferry to Penarth, families with children and picnic hampers, young people laughing and chattering. Then they both spotted Huw hurrying towards them with Annie at his side carrying a basket.

'Mother has packed a picnic for us,' he announced, triumphantly.

'I said that we had made some new friends who were visiting Cardiff and that we were going to show you around, so she's given us some extra treats,' said Annie, breathlessly. 'I mentioned that you were going to the Museum this morning and she was quite impressed. She said that she was glad that I wasn't spending all my time with Molly.'

'Hey, wait for us!' called a voice, and there was Joe running across the road with Luigi. He joined the little group, and burst out, 'I've been and done some ferreting around and I've found out something that may be useful!'

'It's too busy here,' said Huw, calmly. 'Wait till we get to Penarth, then you can tell us everything.'

They scrambled aboard the ferry – a paddle steamer with the name 'Kate' emblazoned on the side – and it set off through the crowded waters of the bay and past the entrance to Penarth Docks where a large, ocean-going ship was being loaded with coal.

When they rounded the headland and sailed towards the landing stage at Penarth, the scene looked strangely familiar to Megan but transformed, like a place seen in a dream. The pier was there but there was no pavilion on it. The beach ahead of them was much more crowded than she remembered it. Rowing boats and yachts bobbed around them on the water and the promenade was busy with people strolling or sitting in groups.

In spite of the warm sun, everyone was dressed in formal clothes, quite unsuited to a day at the seaside. The women wore ankle–length skirts, long–sleeved blouses and hats, decorated with ribbons, artificial flowers and feathers; the men were in trousers and jackets, their heads also covered, in everything from elegant bowler hats to scruffy caps.

Everyone disembarked amongst much shouting and pushing. Once they were all safely onshore, Huw said,

'First we'll have a picnic on the beach and Joe can tell us his news. Then we shall go and look for the photographer's.'

They found themselves a spot where there was flat sand to sit on and Huw opened the picnic basket. There were potted beef sandwiches and little sponge cakes and some lemonade to drink. Joe's face lit up when he saw the spread and he momentarily forgot his eagerness to tell them what he had discovered. Megan slipped off her uncomfortable second-hand boots and stretched out her feet on the muddy sand. Rhys did the same. The cool sand soothed their aching feet and instantly gave them a feeling of well-being. They tucked in eagerly to the picnic.

'We're all ready to listen now, Joe,' said Huw, reaching for another sandwich.

'Well, last night I went along to 'The Packet' and hung around outside till Harry Jenkins and his mates came along. I waited till he had had a few drinks then I decided to impress him. I showed him how good I was at picking pockets and told him that I'd heard that he was pretty clever in that line of business.

'At first he was a bit wary about talking to me but,

in the end, he couldn't stop himself boasting a bit. It seems he gets someone to nick the jewellery for him then sells it to a pawnbroker just off Bute Street who pays him well. It all gets passed on to a big felon from London who sends someone down to Cardiff every few months to collect it.'

There was a tense silence as he continued.

'I said that I could give him a hand, me being so small and nimble and useful with my hands. He said that he would see me tonight and let me know what his next plans are. I thought perhaps we can tip off the rozzers and get him caught in the act.'

Huw was looking worried.

'It all sounds a bit dangerous,' he said, 'but if we could show the police that it's Harry Jenkins who is behind these robberies, perhaps it will help Luigi's brother. Talking of which, we had better go and find the photographer's shop.'

The remains of their picnic were still strewn on the cloth that the food had been wrapped in.

'Perhaps we could take some of this back for Molly and her sisters?' Rhys suggested, feeling a little guilty at the thought of the frugal meals in the O'Sullivan household, and how many sandwiches had vanished into his mouth in the past few minutes. Joe was already stretching out his hand for another cake but, seeing Megan's look of disapproval, he stopped and said,

'Good idea, the little 'uns could do with a bit extra.'

They took the path that led up through the woods to the town. The photographer's was in one of the wider streets and they found it quite easily but the shopkeeper was at the door with keys in his hand and looked as if he was about to lock up the shop.

'I'm sorry,' he said as they approached him, 'You'll have to come back on Monday.'

'Oh please!' pleaded Huw. 'We haven't come to have our photographs taken. We just need to ask you a question.'

'Well, as long as you're quick'

They showed him the photo of Paolo and his girlfriend.

'Ah, yes, I remember taking that photo not long ago,' the man said, 'such an attractive young couple.'

'This boy is looking for his brother, who's in this photo, and we know that his girlfriend lives in Penarth and that her name is Sarah and we wondered if you knew where we could find her.'

The man looked at Luigi and nodded.

'Yes, I see the likeness. I'll have a look in my order book. I seem to remember that the young lady left her name and address, the young man having a rather complicated Italian name. Come on in.'

He searched through his order book, running his finger up the columns of small neat writing.

'Ah, here we are,' he said, 'Miss Sarah Bennett, Clive Place – that's not far from here. You just go up Albert Road and turn right. Number 9.' He wrote out the name and address on a scrap of paper and handed it to Luigi. 'Good luck,' he said, patting his head, 'I hope you find your brother. He was a pleasant young man and such a pretty girl. They seemed a very happy couple.'

Thanking the photographer, they set off in the direction he had indicated. Luigi had forgotten yesterday's set-back and skipped along happily, clutching the photo and the address.

The house was a solidly-built, terrace house, with a small, neat garden in front. The children walked up to the door and Huw pulled on the bell-rope. They heard its jangle echoing around inside the house and after a moment, the door was half-opened by a young girl in a white apron and a frilled white cap. She opened the door slightly wider and wiped her hands on her apron.

'Yes?' she said, curtly, looking them up and down.

'Could we speak to Miss Sarah Bennett, please?' asked Huw.

'Do you know her?'

A voice from inside the house called, 'Who is it, Ellie?'

'Some children to see you, Miss Sarah.'

A young woman appeared behind the maid. Luigi gave a little cry of delight when he saw her.

'It she,' he exclaimed, 'girl in picture.'

The girl, in her turn, gasped when she saw him.

'Who are you?' she asked, 'What do you want?'

And then turning to the maid, she said, 'It's alright, Ellie, you can go.'

Ellie backed away, staring with her mouth open.

Luigi was already waving the photo in front of Sarah.

'This my brother, Paolo,' he said, 'I look for brother.'

She had turned very pale and tears were starting to run down her cheeks.

Then, without warning, she slammed the door shut and they heard the sound of keys turning and bolts being pushed across.

Chapter 22

SARAH'S STORY

They stood for a moment, not knowing whether to leave or stay.

'Well, that did not go very well,' said Huw, despondently. He looked up at the door, firmly closed against them. 'We'd better go, I suppose.' Gloomily, they started back down the path through the woods towards the sea,

Megan put her arm round Luigi's shoulders as the Italian boy tried to stifle a sob. 'Never mind, Luigi, we'll think of something,' she said, soothingly.

Suddenly, they heard hurried footsteps behind them and a breathless voice called, 'Wait, please wait.' They turned to see Sarah, her face pink from running and a straw hat decorated with ribbons crammed onto her fair hair.

'I do so want to speak to you,' she panted. 'I am sorry I closed the door like that – it was the shock of hearing Paolo's name. Do you know where he is? Where did you find that picture? Are you really Paolo's brother? He talked of you often. You look so much like him. Let us sit on this seat while we talk.'

Her words poured out in a torrent as she led them to a little bench, half hidden in the shrubbery. Megan and Rhys told her how they had found Luigi and been given the photo by Mrs. Probert.

Sarah nodded.

'Yes, that was such a happy day when we went to the photographer's together,' she said. 'I had met Paolo one day when I was walking along the cliffs with Ellie, our maid. He caught my hat for me when it blew away. He told me that he had come to Wales to earn money to send to his mother and brother in Italy and that when he had enough he would pay for them to come here as well. After that we met many times, sometimes on the cliffs and sometimes when I was on the way to chapel. He told me that he had met someone called Harry who said that he would help him make his fortune and … well, it was odd because after that, he did not come to see me so often.

'Then, one day, he appeared when I was walking along the cliffs and he looked terrible. He said that he had done a very bad thing and that he needed to go away until he could put it right. He went off along the path towards Lavernock Point and I haven't seen him since then. Paolo used to like going there because he had read in the newspaper about an inventor, an Italian gentleman, who made some important experiments there.'

'That would be Marconi then,' said Megan, remembering the newspaper cutting which Paolo had kept.

'That's right,' said Sarah. 'And he told me about a

farm he had seen along there, not far from the cliff edge, which looked like an ideal place to live and that some day, when he had made his fortune, we would buy somewhere like that and bring up a family.'

A large tear rolled down her cheek.

Megan placed her hand on one of Sarah's.

'Don't be so sad,' she said, 'We may be able to help you.'

She hesitated, unwilling to cause Sarah even more distress by telling her about the robbery. Luigi had been listening intently, trying to follow the conversation.

'Bad man,' he blurted out, shaking his head, 'He say my brother thief. But Paolo good boy. He not do that.'

Sarah gasped and put her hand to her mouth.

'What are you saying?' Her voice was fearful. 'Was he a thief? Is he in jail?'

'You mentioned a man called Harry,' said Huw, 'and Joe knows this man. It looks as if he had some sort of evil influence on Paolo and forced him to steal a necklace from his landlady. That's why he disappeared – he must have felt guilty about it straightway.'

'But Joe has been finding more out about this Harry Jenkins and we think we may be able to clear Paolo's name,' Megan continued hurriedly, seeing the shocked look on Sarah's face.

'Well,' said Sarah, wiping her eyes with a delicate

lace-edged handkerchief that she took from her pocket. 'You children have been very busy. I don't really understand who you are or why you are doing this but it makes me feel better to know that there are such kind people in the world. I hope you discover the truth.'

She stood up. 'I need to go back now or I shall be in trouble. Please come and tell me if you have any news.' With that, she got up to leave but before she went, she bent down and planted a quick kiss on Luigi's cheek.

'You look so much like your brother,' she said, blushing slightly. 'I do hope that we shall be able to find Paolo and sort everything out.'

She adjusted her hat, shook hands with each of them and hurried back up towards the town.

Chapter 23

THE ICE-CREAM SELLER

As they walked back along the sea-front towards the ferry, Rhys noticed that a number of people were eating delicious looking ice-creams and his food radar soon homed in on the person who was selling them.

'Megs,' he said, 'we still have some of the money that old man at the museum gave us this morning, don't we? We could buy an ice-cream each for us all.'

Luigi had also noticed the ice-creams. He suddenly raced across the promenade, shouting excitedly.

'Italiano. E gelato italiano!' He had caught sight of the name painted over the shop–front – Moretti's Italian Ice-Cream.

The lady behind the counter heard her native language through the hubbub of the crowd around the shop.

'Parli italiano? Sei italiano?' she asked, and Luigi answered that yes, he was Italian and launched into a stream of the language, hardly stopping for breath. The children heard Paolo's name being mentioned and the man who was serving out the ice-cream came over with his scoop still in his hand and joined in.

'What are they saying?' said Rhys, 'I hope they don't forget our ice-creams.'

The man came round from behind the counter and said to the children, 'This boy here says that he is looking for his brother. We knew this Paolo. He came here many times, sometimes alone and once or twice with his young lady. Bellisima, a beautiful young lady, and such a nice young man, molto simpatico, molto corretto, very nice, very honest. This boy here, he look like his brother.'

'Do you know where he is now?' asked Huw.

The ice-cream seller shook his head.

'He had some trouble, he would not tell us what it was but he was very sad, very – how do you say? – very ashamed. He came to say 'Goodbye'. He said that he was going to look for work at the quarry.'

The lady spoke again in Italian to her husband, then said in English to the children, 'You come for ice-creams? We give you for sake of Paolo and because you good children to help Luigi.'

When he had served them all, the ice-cream seller spoke to Luigi again then said to the children,

'I say to him to come and tell me if he find his brother. If you go to the quarry, perhaps he will be there. Good luck.'

'We go now and find Paolo?' Luigi tugged at Megan's sleeve.

'No, no, it's too late today – we need to catch the ferry back to the docks,' Huw said.

Luigi looked unwilling to leave but Megan took his hand and said, 'Come on Luigi, at least we know

now where your brother might be. We'll come back tomorrow.'

'Yes,' Huw agreed, 'and we'll walk along the cliff path towards the quarry and perhaps ask at the farm too.'

And they crossed once again, over the water, to the bustling, heaving docks of Cardiff, excited at the prospect of what the next day might bring.

Chapter 24

THE PLAN DEVELOPS

The next morning, Megan and Rhys woke late.

'Phew, I really need a shower,' whispered Megan to Rhys as they washed quickly, and none too thoroughly, in the cold water from the pump in the yard, and dried themselves on the rough piece of grubby towel that everyone used. 'And I wish I could have some clean clothes. These really smell.'

'Well, everything else smells too!' grinned Rhys, 'So don't worry. Anyway, I think it's quite cool not having to worry about washing all the time'

They hurried downstairs, and while they were gnawing on the stale bread which was all there was for breakfast, Joe wandered into the kitchen, yawning and scratching his head. He'd been out for the best part of the night, intent on his mission to winkle out more information about Harry Jenkins.

'Ready for action?' he said, 'I had a very successful night's ferreting and I have some information that we may be able to use. I'll tell you when we meet Huw.'

Molly came in from the scullery and heard his words. She was about to give him an earful about his reckless behaviour, but Megan reassured her quickly that Joe's help was essential. Joe seemed to puff up with pride at the praise and he gave Molly a cheeky wink.

'Get away with you, Joe O'Sullivan' she said, stretching out her arm to cuff him round the ears. But Joe was too fast for her and was already out through the door.

Just before midday, they were all sitting beside the water at the Pier Head.

'So, Joe, tell us the latest,' said Huw.

'Well, Harry is planning another robbery for tonight and will take me along too. So, he will be going to the pawnbroker's tomorrow and I shall be with him. That will be a good time to shop him to the police.'

'But how will we be able to get them to take us seriously?' asked Megan, 'They'll think we're just making up stories and wasting their time.'

'I've been thinking about that,' said Huw. 'My father had a good friend who is a policeman. He lives a few doors away from us. When my father died, he said to my mother that if ever any of us needed help at any time, we could go to him. He's a kind man and I think that he would listen to me.'

'But if we tell the police, won't Paolo be in trouble because he was the one who took Mrs. Probert's necklace?' said Rhys.

'Harry happened to tell me the pawnbroker has quite a stash of jewellery at the moment but that the big man himself, the ringleader from London will be coming down quite soon to collect it and check on the whole operation. So the necklace that Luigi's brother took from the old girl in the lodging house is probably still in his shop,' explained Joe.

'Mrs. Probert would be really pleased to have it back and she did seem to like Paolo – she said he was such a nice, polite boy. I'm sure that she'd speak up for him,' said Megan.

'But first we need to find Paolo,' said Huw, 'so let's not waste any more time.'

'Can I come too?' asked Joe, 'There's nothing else I can do – Harry'll be sleeping till dark.'

'Let him come – we can pay the ferry fare for him – we still have some of our money from yesterday,' said Megan.

'And I have some apples and bread and cheese,' said Huw, 'We'll eat them on the beach.'

And they boarded the ferry once more.

Chapter 25

ALONG THE CLIFFS

That Sunday, it seemed that most of the population of Penarth and the surrounding area had gone down to the sea-front to enjoy the fine weather. The path up to the cliffs too was thronged with people dressed in their Sunday best. Ladies with parasols wearing pastel-coloured satin dresses with nipped-in waists strolled in a leisurely fashion, with elegantly suited gentlemen in bowler hats or boaters. A small boy, dressed in a sailor suit bowled a hoop along the cliff path. The girls of Megan's age wore dresses with frills and flounces and brightly coloured sashes. Staring at them as they passed, she realized how shabby she must look

The children continued along the cliff-top path which became rougher and more overgrown as they drew further away from the town. The sound of voices and the hubbub of the sea-front were left behind and all they could hear now was the screaming of the gulls, the gentle sighing of the sea and the rustle of the long grasses in the breeze.

'This is nice,' said Joe, 'It makes you feel that life ain't so bad after all.'

'*Isn't* so bad,' Megan corrected him. 'You know,

Joe, life really isn't *so* bad because even if you don't have much money, you can go to school for free and if you went to school and learnt to read and write, you would be able to get a good job, like Huw.'

'I dunno,' said Joe, shrugging his shoulders, 'I can't do sums and figure out those ABC letters.'

'But you're really clever Joe. You know lots of things already that we don't know – like how to look after yourself on the streets. I bet you'd learn to read and write really quickly and once you can read, you can find out all sorts of interesting things about the world, and about history and how things work, and there are lots of books of amazing, exciting stories, aren't there, Huw?'

Huw agreed enthusiastically. 'You could borrow some of my books, Joe – if you wanted.'

'Well, you never know,' Joe said, thoughtfully. 'I might even try it once we've finished this bit of business.'

Not far from the cliff edge stood a cluster of low white-washed buildings surrounded by fields.

'That must be the farm Sarah told us about,' said Megan.

'I can see why Luigi's brother liked the look of it,' said Joe, 'It would be a treat and no mistake to live out here in the fresh air and watch the boats go by in the distance without all the noise and dust and the stink of the docks.'

'We'll go and talk to the farmer,' said Huw. They

crossed a field of sheep and overgrown lambs and opened the gate into the farm-yard. A black and white dog leapt in front of them, barking frantically. To their relief they saw that it was chained to a kennel but it was straining to the length of its tether and making a fearful din. Two little children were playing outside the door and one of them jumped up and ran inside calling out in Welsh. A youngish woman appeared, wiping her hands on her apron and frowned when she saw the children.

Huw stepped forward but before he could say anything, a tall man came round the side of the house. He was dressed in dirty work clothes and was carrying a large stick, which he waved fiercely in their direction. Another dog followed at his heels, growling menacingly and baring its teeth at them.

They all took an instinctive step back. What was he going to do?

'Go away,' he shouted, 'I'll have no beggars here. Get off my land or I'll set the dogs on you.'

He strode towards them, with an angry look in his eyes. They turned and fled.

Chapter 26

SUCCESS!

The children ran back across the field as fast as they could. Once they were near the gate, Huw turned and looked back.

'Slow down,' he called to the others. 'Don't worry, he's not chasing us.'

Megan, Rhys and Joe came to a halt and stood still, panting and out of breath.

'Jesus,' gasped Joe, 'it's more dangerous out here than it is down by the docks. Those dogs were like monsters!'

They all laughed nervously, relieved to have got safely away.

'Let's go and get the boat back now,' continued Joe.

'But I shall have to go to work tomorrow,' said Huw, reluctantly, 'so while we're here, can't we just walk out to Lavernock Point? I'd like to see the place where Signor Marconi conducted his experiments.'

'We've still got to walk all the way back to the landing-stage remember,' Rhys said, grumpily, kicking at a stone on the path.

'Don't be so miserable,' said Megan, 'it's only just over there.'

She took Luigi's hand and smiled encouragingly. 'We'll sit down and have a rest when we get to the cliff edge,' she said, cheerfully.

When they arrived at the extremity of the headland, Huw said, 'Marconi must have been sending his telegraphs near here. There's the island of Flat Holm across there.'

'Look – there's the path down to the beach,' said Megan. 'Let's go down and sit on the rocks. We can take our shoes off and paddle in the rock pools to cool our feet before we walk back.'

The walk took just a few moments. Megan settled down on the nearest rock and was already pulling off her uncomfortable boots when she noticed that Luigi was standing stock still staring along the beach. On another rock, a short distance away, and looking out to sea, there was a seated figure.

'Paolo?' said Luigi, hesitantly, 'Is Paolo?!' and he started to run, across the beach.

'Wait, Luigi,' said Megan, 'it might not be him!'

But Luigi was stumbling over the rocks, shouting his brother's name and when the person leapt up and spun round to face them, Megan saw a slender, dark-haired young man who looked just like an older version of Luigi.

'Luigi?' he said, with an incredulous look on his face. 'Non lo credo!'

A torrent of Italian poured out of Luigi as he staggered the last few steps towards his brother and flung his arms round him. The young man hugged him in return and when he looked towards the children, tears were rolling down his cheeks. Luigi, his face buried in his brother's rough shirt, was still talking breathlessly, his words punctuated by deep sobs. Huw and the others stood, awkwardly, a short way off, unsure what to do or say. After a few minutes, Luigi seemed to run out of breath and Paolo managed to free himself from his younger brother's grasp sufficiently to turn his attention to the children.

'Grazie mille,' he said, ' A thousand thank yous for bringing my brother here. He says that you were very kind to him – like angels.' Then his voice turned a little sad. 'But I am not a good person, you know. I did a terrible thing and I cannot look after him now – Luigi needs a good home and I can do nothing.'

'We know what you did and that it was Harry Jenkins' fault, not yours,' said Huw, stretching out his hand towards Paolo, 'How do you do? I am Huw Morgan. This is Joe and these two are Megan and Rhys. They were the ones who found Luigi in the first place. And don't worry. We have a plan to help you restore your good name.'

Paolo looked from one to another of them with a slightly stunned expression on his face. He brushed the tears from his cheek and ran his hand through his hair.

'Let's all sit down,' suggested Megan, 'then we can explain everything.'

Paolo listened intently to their story, and to the plan they had in mind. When they had finished, he said,

'If the necklace is still at the pawnbroker's, I can make up for the bad thing I did by giving it back to Mrs. Probert.'

'What does the necklace look like?' asked Megan.

'It is gold and set with pearls and garnets. It had belonged to Mrs. Probert's mother – she was very proud of it. But you must not put yourselves in danger.'

'Don't you worry,' said Joe, 'I'll make sure that these respectable citizens don't get into no trouble. By the way, that young lady of yours is quite a stunner and very sweet on you too. I'd get back together with her pronto, if I was you.' And he gave Paolo a cheeky wink.

'Sarah, you've seen Sarah?' Paolo turned pale.

'Yes, and she's very worried about you,' said Megan.

Paolo sighed. 'It's all such a mess,' he said, shaking his head. 'I have been so stupid.'

'Oh, my goodness! We have to get back,' said Huw, jumping up suddenly. 'The sun is quite low now so it must be getting late.'

Luigi was still clinging to his brother.

'I think it is best if Luigi comes with you for now,' Paolo said, trying to prize his brother's fingers off his shirt. 'I live at the farm back there. I sleep in the barn and work for the farmer, when I am not at the quarry.'

'The scary farm with the angry farmer and the mad dogs?' said Rhys. 'I wouldn't want to live there.'

'They are good people,' Paolo said, 'They have been kind to me but living out here by themselves, they are nervous of strangers. They probably thought that you were gypsies. I must admit that Luigi looks like a, how do you say – ragamuffin?' He gave Luigi a playful poke and said something to him in Italian that made the young boy laugh.

'Tomorrow, I shall walk along the cliffs towards Penarth when I leave work in the quarry, to look out for you all,' said Paolo. 'Ciao, Luigi, a domani – see you all tomorrow and good luck!'

Chapter 27

THE ARTIST ON THE CLIFFS

The path seemed longer and rougher on the way back to the ferry. Megan was thinking gloomily that, although they had found Paolo – and she felt pleased about that – they were no nearer to finding a way of getting back to their own time. And all of a sudden she was missing home a lot. Rhys and Joe were dragging their feet and although Luigi was humming happily to himself, he was dawdling behind. However, Huw was still in good spirits.

'Well, that was a successful day's work!' he declared brightly. But Megan just sighed and said quietly, 'Don't forget that *we* need to find a way of getting back home too.'

Rhys saw the look in her eyes and came to join her. He linked his arm in hers – after all, there was no-one from his class there to see – and said, 'Don't worry, Megs. We've helped Luigi now. That's what Mr. Bartholomew said we had to do. So perhaps now we'll discover a way home really quickly.'

Megan gave a wan smile. He prodded her gently in the ribs and said 'Don't be a grumpy cat. Last one to the bench is a soggy cornflake!' and sped off, leaving her giggling, despite her worry.

Just ahead of them near the path there was a small group of people and, as they drew nearer, they could see that one man was sitting on a stool in front of an easel on which was propped a half-finished painting. A lady with a parasol stood nearby. But Megan's attention was attracted to the elderly man who was standing talking to the couple.

'Mr. Bartholomew!' she gasped, and started to run, waving her arms and calling out, 'Don't go, we need to speak to you.' But before she reached him, she saw him take off his hat, give a slight bow and stride rapidly away towards the town. Megan ran as fast as she could, still calling his name and he hesitated, turned slightly and waved his stick towards her, in greeting. Then, he was swallowed up in a noisy group of young people who were strolling along the path. Megan became entangled in the laughing, chattering crowd and when she managed to extricate herself, Mr. Bartholomew had already disappeared from view.

She stood staring around her, then slowly made her way back up to the spot where the artist was painting his picture.

'Hey, Megs, why did you rush off like that? You went way past the bench.'

Megan came to a halt, her face flushed and her shoulders heaving.

'I just saw Mr. Bartholomew again,' she said. 'He

was talking to the artist, then he just vanished into the crowd.'

Her lip trembled. Twice now she had lost him. Would there be another chance? How could she have been so unlucky?

'Hey! Look at this!' called Rhys, distracting her as he noticed her quivering lip. He pointed at the canvas, 'Don't you have a picture like that in your house?'

She looked over the man's shoulder at the painting. It was not finished yet, but it showed the curve of the cliff and the rocky beach below. Rhys was right. It was just like the one her Grandma had given to her mother for Christmas.

'That painting's in the museum!' she exclaimed. 'Grandma showed it to me when she took me in there once.'

'Je crois qu'il faut rentrer. We must go, Alfred.' The lady was twirling her parasol impatiently and eyeing the children in a suspicious manner.

'Alors, je reviens demain,' said the man, wiping his hands on a red cloth that he pulled out of his trouser pocket.

'They're speaking French,' Megan whispered to Rhys.

'Well, you're good at French, aren't you?' answered Rhys, 'Say something to them.'

'My mind's gone blank. You say something,' hissed Megan.

'Well, I only know the words for the things in my

pencil case,' said Rhys, 'and what use is that? I could ask him for a pencil or pen, but that's all!'

'What's the matter with you kids? Why have we all stopped?' It was Joe, trying to get a closer look at the painting. The lady shooed him away and shook the painter's arm to hurry him along in his preparations to leave.

'I think I heard him say 'demain.' That means 'tomorrow', doesn't it?' said Huw, 'I have studied a little French from a book I found in the public library. So perhaps he's coming back tomorrow to finish his picture. You can come and look for him then. We really need to catch the next boat. It looks as if it's going to rain.' The wind had picked up and dark clouds were gathering over the hills.

Megan turned away reluctantly but then she had second thoughts and ran back to the French couple.

'Er, excusez–moi,' she started, and then lapsing into slow English, 'Will you be here tomorrow?'

The man shrugged his shoulders, as he covered the picture with a cloth.

'Oui, Mademoiselle, perhaps I come tomorrow.'

'Did you know that man who was talking to you just now? Do you know where I can find him?'

'You have many questions,' said the man. 'I do not know …'

The lady cut him short. 'Viens,' she said curtly, giving Megan an unfriendly look. 'Come. We leave.' A few drops of rain were starting to fall. The artist hesitated then smiled at Megan, ignoring the lady's exasperated sighs.

'I am recently acquainted with the man of whom you speak, Mademoiselle. I think that his name is Mr. Bartholomew. He speaks excellent French and he seems to know many things about art. He said that he would like to come and see the other paintings that I have made here. Now I must go, au revoir.'

'Au revoir,' said Megan and ran as fast as she could to catch up with the others, her head spinning with possibilities.

She hardly dared believe that, perhaps, there was the slightest chance that this might be the painting they had been so desperate to find.

Chapter 28

ANOTHER SURPRISE

By the time they all stumbled off the ferry at the Pier Head, the rain was falling steadily and after a few minutes, they were soaked through.

'I'll walk back along with you all,' said Huw. 'And we'll run over our plans for tomorrow.'

'Well,' said Joe, 'if Harry does the job tonight, like he said, he'll want to take his pickings to the pawnbroker's tomorrow as soon as he gets up, which is not very early as I told you. I'll come and let you know as soon as I'm sure of the time and you lot will have to be ready to come with the law so he can be caught red-handed.'

'And I'll have to go and talk to Sergeant Price first thing tomorrow morning,' said Huw, 'and hope that I can persuade him to come with us.'

There was no sign of Molly or her brothers and sisters in her street and when they went along the alley at the side of the house and through the yard, it all seemed strangely quiet. Joe tried to turn the doorknob but the door did not budge. He peered in through the dirty glass pane.

'I can't see anyone there,' he said, frowning. 'That's strange. We'd better try the front door.'

They retraced their footsteps and Joe tried the front door but that was locked too. While they were knocking and rattling the handle, a swarthy-faced woman in a faded print dress and ragged shawl, who had stopped on the opposite side of the street, called across to them,

'You're wastin' your time, Joe. Where you bin? There's nobody there. They've all been carted off.'

'What?' said Huw, shocked.

The woman shuffled across the road.

'The police came and arrested Mrs. O'Sullivan,' she said, with relish, 'and the kids was all taken off to the children's home in Moira Terrace seeing as they could not be left by themselves.'

'Oh no, that's terrible!' exclaimed Megan, imagining seeing her own mother taken away by the police.

'That's what happens when yer gets yerself mixed up with all manner of no–goods,' the woman muttered, and she went in and slammed the door.

Megan was horrified. Seeing that she was so upset, Huw said,

'Don't worry, Megan. This happens, you know. But Molly and the little kids will be looked after much better in the children's home than they were here.'

'But what about our bags?' exclaimed Rhys, suddenly. Their back–packs were still stowed away under the bed upstairs, and in them were their own clothes and all their stuff. 'We need our bags, Megs!'

There was a moment of quiet panic as they contemplated the fact that everything they owned was locked away in the house,

Then Joe jumped up from the doorstep where he had perched himself. 'Don't you be worrying about that,' he said. 'The front door might be locked – but that's never stopped Joe O'Sullivan! Wait here!'

He sprinted back down the alley-way at the side of the house and was soon back with the two grimy bundles of belongings. He winked at Megan and Rhys. 'Here are your two precious bundles,' he announced with a bow. 'That back window never did shut properly!'

'Listen,' said Huw, taking charge of the situation, 'You must all come home with me. You're soaking wet all of you, and you can't stay here. I am sure that Mother will not turn you away. You too, Joe. But you'd better be careful what you're saying at my house.'

'I'll behave myself, don't you worry,' said Joe, seeing the prospect of a meal on the horizon, 'but I'll need to slip out later to go and meet Harry, remember.'

A few minutes later, Mrs. Morgan opened the front door and stared in surprise at the little dripping huddle of children on the step.

'Where on earth have you been? And who are these waifs and strays with you?' she said. Annie was behind her trying desperately to see what was happening.

'I know them, Mam,' she said 'Their names are

Megan and Rhys and the little one is Luigi. They were all staying at Molly's house.'

'But when we went back there just now it was all locked up,' said Huw. ' Apparently Molly's mother has been arrested and the kids have all been taken to the children's home – except Joe here, because he was with us.'

Mrs. Morgan was looking puzzled but her natural kindness took over and she exclaimed, 'Oh, you poor things. You're all soaked. You had better come in.' She shepherded them into the living room. 'I'll go and find some of your old clothes for them to put on. I had a bundle ready to take to St. Mary's for the orphans. And I'll put the water on to heat up for the tin bath in the kitchen.'

Mrs. Morgan eyed Megan and Rhys suspiciously each time she went past them and when her eyes alighted on Joe, she frowned. She had a quiet word with her son in the hallway.

'You have always been a good boy, Huw, but it does seem rather strange that you suddenly bring these urchins home. And why did you have one of those dreadful O'Sullivan children with you?'

'Luigi comes from Italy and Megan and Rhys have been helping him to find his older brother,' whispered Huw. 'Joe O'Sullivan has just been really helpful. We are not doing anything wrong, Please, Mother, trust me.'

Mrs. Morgan shook her head and sighed.

Annie hung on her arm and looked pleadingly into her eyes.

'Come on, Mam,' she said, 'You always say that we should be good Christians and be generous to those who have less than we do.'

Mrs. Morgan sighed again as she led Megan into the kitchen and closed the door, saying,

'Well, you'd better get those wet clothes off you, young lady, or you'll catch your death of cold.'

Megan quickly undressed and climbed into the tin bath. It was lovely being able to immerse her body in warm water again. She noticed that Mrs. Morgan was looking curiously at the clothes she had taken off, especially her Marks and Spencer knickers decorated with pink hearts and she hoped that she would not ask her any awkward questions. She put on the old clothes of Annie's that Mrs. Morgan handed her. They were rather tight and faded from much use but they were dry and clean and smelt fresh.

'Take Megan into the sitting-room, Annie,' said Mrs. Morgan, ushering the boys into the kitchen in a determined fashion. They looked horrified at the prospect of shedding their clothes and getting into the tin bath, and Joe was on the point of escaping, but Huw encouraged them by saying, 'Hurry up, then we can have our supper.'

Once they were all washed and re-clothed, Mrs. Morgan seated them round the scrubbed wooden table and placed a variety of well-laden plates and dishes in front of them. There were thick slices of bread with cheese and jam and fruit cake baked that day.

Clean, comfortable and well-fed, Megan felt her eyes beginning to close and, through drooping eyelids, looked around the table. Luigi was leaning heavily against Annie and seemed to have fallen asleep with the remains of his cake still in his hand; Joe was yawning; and Rhys appeared to be nodding off. Mrs. Morgan had also noticed the children's sleepiness.

'Well, I think it's bed for all of you now,' she said, 'and in the morning we'll decide what to do. Annie, come and help me get down some extra blankets and pillows.'

Once Mrs. Morgan was out of the room Joe said, 'I wouldn't mind a bit of a kip before I go and meet Harry. Trouble is if I'm nice and comfy, I might sleep till kingdom come.'

'Don't worry, I'll stay awake. I want to read my book,' said Huw, 'I'll wake you up after Mam's gone to bed and let you out through the kitchen door.'

Chapter 29

TIME FOR ACTION

'Megan, Megan, wake up!'

Megan opened her eyes and blinked in the bright sunlight. Annie was sitting on the bed in front of her, already dressed and with her hair neatly plaited.

'Mam said to let you and Rhys sleep as long as you wanted as you seemed so tired, but I need to talk to you.'

'What's the matter?' Megan said, rubbing her eyes. 'Is Rhys alright?'

'Yes, he's still asleep and so is Luigi.' She lowered her voice. 'Joe has gone during the night to find Harry, as we planned. Mam was very cross when she found that he'd disappeared and said that it was just as she expected and that he'd tricked her into giving him some decent clothes and a good meal. Huw left early – he told Mam that he has a lot of work to do but he's going to call on Sergeant Price and he'll meet us at the Pier Head later. Now, you go and wake Rhys and Luigi and I'll help Mam in the kitchen.'

Rhys pulled the sheet over his head and groaned when Megan called him. Finally, he struggled to a sitting position, rubbed his head vigorously and blinked his eyes.

'Oh no, we're still here,' he said, 'I dreamt that I was back home and that all this had been a dream.'

'Well, the only way we're going to get back home is if you get up and get dressed. Wake Luigi up as well.'

During breakfast, it was clear that Mrs. Morgan had questions she wanted to ask Megan and Rhys but the children managed to distract her by recounting the story of Luigi and his search for his brother, without mentioning the matter of the robbery. But when they had finished, she said,

'So if you have found his brother, why is he still with you? And where exactly do you two come from?'

Annie jumped up from her seat and said, 'We'll tell you later when Huw comes home. Don't you need to go out to do the shopping, Mam? Megan and I will do the chores. Then, if you let us take some apples and biscuits, we can all go and play over the wall and stay out till supper and not 'get in your hair' as you say.'

Mrs. Morgan sighed, 'I suppose so,' she said, 'A pity that little rascal Joe escaped. I could have taken him along to the Children's Home to join the others.'

She hung her pinafore on a hook behind the door, took down a shopping basket and, giving Annie a quick kiss on the cheek, finally disappeared through the back door.

'Phew,' said Annie, 'come on you boys. You can help too.'

When they arrived at the Pier Head they spotted Joe perched on one of the bollards. He waved cheerfully when he saw them.

Huw arrived a few minutes later, looking flushed and a little anxious.

'So, Joe?' he asked, urgently.

'Well, Harry did the job and I went along with him to help. He's going to take the jewellery to the pawnbroker's in Humphrey Street this afternoon and I'll be with him. You lot will need to be there to stop him escaping. There's a back entrance to the shop so you'll need to cover that too.'

'Right, that sounds like a good plan. You know how to get to Humphrey Street, don't you Annie? I'll have to go to the Police Station and find Sergeant Price,' said Huw.

'What did he say when you spoke to him?' asked Megan.

'Fortunately, he knew of Harry Jenkins. He said that the police had had their eye on him for some time but had not been able to pin anything definite on him so he was interested in our plan but he said that we should have gone to a grown-up and not tried to sort things out ourselves.'

'Grown-ups,' said Joe, scornfully, 'they just try and tell you what to do and if you don't do it they beat you.'

'They also look after you and give you a tasty supper and a comfortable bed, like Mrs. Morgan did last night,' said Megan, frowning at him, '*and* she's given us some apples and biscuits to eat. Shall we have them now, Annie, before we go to the pawnbroker's shop?'

'But let's move away from here,' said Huw, looking around him uneasily. 'I had to tell Mr. Thomas, the boss, that Mam was unwell and needed me to help her. I ought to make sure that I am not seen by the other boys from the office when they come down here to eat their lunch.'

So, they went over to the loading dock and sat on a crate, watching the boats while they ate. All around them was the sound of creaking rigging, chugging engines and shouted commands, while a haze of coal dust hung in the summer air, and the gulls wheeled and screeched overhead. Time passed enjoyably.

Suddenly Huw sprang up, brushing the crumbs from his trousers.

'Right,' he said, 'Time for action everybody. But do be careful. Harry Jenkins sounds like a bad lot and he will not let a few little kids stand in his way.'

Chapter 30

THE PAWNBROKER'S

They said goodbye to Huw and Joe and set off towards the pawnbroker's.

'I've been thinking about what we should do,' said Megan. 'Rhys, you go round to the back entrance of the shop with Annie to stop Harry making a run for it, and I'll keep watch at the front, with Luigi, and send him to tell you when we see Joe and Harry coming.' Rhys agreed readily, excited at the prospect of playing such a key part in what sounded like an adventure of a lifetime.

Annie led the way through streets of small, shabby terraced houses with dark, alley ways between them at intervals. They passed groups of sailors laughing loudly and talking in strange languages. and men wearing the bright robes of African countries. Everywhere there were ragged children, playing on doorsteps and in the gutters.

'I think the place is just along here,' said Annie, turning into a cul-de-sac.

The pawnbroker's was a dingy little shop. In the dusty window, there was a pile of plates of varying sizes, some fanned out collections of tarnished silver spoons, and piles of what looked like old sheets and blankets. On the door, a faded hand-written notice said 'Closed'. Fortunately, there was no-one around apart from a small knot of children playing beside the tall brick wall that blocked off the end of the street.

Megan and Luigi sat down on the bottom step of a house opposite the shop while Annie and Rhys slipped quickly into the alley-way.

Ten minutes passed slowly.

A sour-faced woman came out of her front door and shooed the children off the step. Megan pulled Luigi out of her way and just as she was looking around for somewhere else to position herself, she saw two figures turn the corner of the street, a man and a boy. As they came nearer, Megan's heart started to beat faster. She knew that she should not stare at them but could not resist the temptation to cast a rapid glance at Joe and his companion as they approached. Harry was solidly built with a square face and slicked-back black hair. His shifty eyes scanned the street but passed over Megan and Luigi without registering any reaction. He sidled up to the door and rapped twice with his knuckles. An invisible hand opened it but before the two of them slipped inside, Joe looked straight at Megan and winked.

'Luigi, go down the alley to Annie and Rhys and tell them that Joe and Harry are in the shop,' Megan urged, giving the Italian boy a shove in the right direction.

'Si, si,' whispered Luigi, excitedly, 'I go.'

Megan looked anxiously back along the street but there was no sign of Huw and Sergeant Price. Where could they be? There was not a moment to lose, and they should have been there.

Just as she was beginning to despair, a group of figures turned the corner. It was Huw flanked by the burly, reassuring shapes of two policemen. She waved energetically and the two broke into a run, or rather, a breathless trot as they came nearer. They looked hot and red-faced in their uniforms with their tightly-buttoned jackets and helmets. The younger of the two policemen slipped into the alley-way and the older one, who Megan thought must be Sergeant Price, knocked sharply on the door of the shop and then gave it a hefty push with his shoulder. They heard a commotion inside and suddenly the door burst open and Sergeant Price half fell inside, almost on top of Joe who had slipped back the bolts. Megan and Huw rushed in after him.

The pawnbroker, a small, skinny, frightened-looking man in a velvet skull cap and a dusty jacket, was cowering behind the counter as Harry scrambled over it, scattering the piles of crockery and bed-linen that were stacked there. At the same moment, the young policeman, followed by Annie, Rhys and Luigi burst into the shop through the back door. Harry ran full tilt into the policeman, knocking him to the ground and tried to dodge the children but they were quicker than he was. Annie hung onto his jacket and while he was struggling to pull free, Rhys gave him a hearty kick on the ankle which made him yell out in pain, and Luigi slammed shut the back door and pushed the bolt across.

By this time, the young police constable was on his feet again and Sergeant Price was with him behind the counter. Between them, they grabbed Harry firmly.

'I am arresting you in the name of the Law on suspicion of stealing various items of jewellery and selling them to this gentleman,' Sergeant Price intoned, while the young police constable clapped a set of handcuffs on Harry's wrists, and turning to the pawn-broker, he said, 'And you Mr. Moses will also need to accompany me to the police-station and answer a few questions. If you come quietly, I shall not need to cuff you.'

'I'll tell you everything you need to know,' Mr. Moses whined. 'It's not my fault. I was forced to take the stuff. I was threatened. It wasn't just Harry Jenkins here, the other bloke from London said …'

'Shut up, you fool,' snapped Harry, struggling to free himself.

'Too late, Harry' said Sergeant Price, 'we already have an idea of who's behind this whole set-up and I have a list here of all the items of jewellery that have been stolen in the last six months.'

'He keeps the valuable stuff in a locked drawer under his counter,' volunteered Joe, pointing to the place.

Sergeant Price was already rattling the drawer. 'I'll have the key for this if you please, Mr. Moses,' he said, scowling at the pawnbroker who was still cowering behind the counter, looking nervously from the policeman to Harry and back again. With trembling fingers he fumbled in his pocket and brought out a small key, while Harry muttered curses under his breath.

'Well, well,' said Sergeant Price, as he peered into the drawer, 'these look like the items that were stolen last night.'

The children were crowding round, trying to see what was there.

'And that looks like the necklace that Paolo described!' said Huw. 'Look, it has garnets and pearls set in it. So it is still here!'

Sergeant Price was consulting his list. ''Mrs. Probert, 44 Adelaide Street, reported the theft of a necklace, set with garnets and pearls' I think you could be right, young man.'

Suddenly, there was an urgent knock on the door and it opened to reveal another policeman who looked startlingly similar to the other two with his tightly buttoned jacket, helmet and black moustache.

'Ah, PC Davies,' said Sergeant Price, 'just as well I asked you to call in here. You can help PC Jones escort these two gentlemen to the station. I need to make sure that these children get back safely to their homes.'

'We'll be alright, sir,' said Huw, 'you don't need to trouble yourself.'

'Well, I should like to have a word with your mother,' said the Sergeant, 'and your parents too,' he added, looking at the semi-circle of children surrounding him. 'It's all turned out very well but it could have been very different. You should not be wandering so freely in the streets and taking the law into your own hands however good the cause.'

Harry and the pawnbroker were escorted from the shop by the two policemen. Outside there was a closed carriage waiting to take them to the police-station. A small crowd had gathered, alerted to the incident by the commotion in the pawnbrokers and the sight of the police. Sergeant Price and the children followed the carriage along the street on foot. Joe was fidgeting uneasily.

'I don't need to come with you, sir,' he said.

'Aren't you one of those O'Sullivan children?' said Sergeant Price, 'I recognize the red hair. I've heard that your sisters and baby brother were taken to Dr Barnardo's yesterday.'

'He spent the night with us,' explained Huw, 'because when we got back to their house there was no-one there. I'm sure that my mother will take him along to the children's home later.'

Joe opened his mouth to protest but then glanced at Megan and thought better of it.

'What about the rest of you?'

'Luigi here is Paolo's younger brother. He stayed with us as well last night.'

'And you two?' Megan and Rhys were doing their best to look inconspicuous.

'They are staying with us too,' said Huw, blushing slightly.

'They're our cousins,' Annie added, helpfully, while Huw frowned at her.

'Well, you must have had a full house,' commented the Sergeant with a smile. 'We'd better all go back there now I think.'

Chapter 31

HAPPY ENDINGS?

Mrs. Morgan opened the door, looking flustered and anxious.

'Now, don't worry, Mrs. Morgan,' Sergeant Price said, reassuringly, 'I would just like to have a quick word with you about these young people.'

'Do come in, Sergeant Price. I hope they haven't got themselves into any trouble, I'm sure that I have tried to bring my two up to act in a Christian manner but it is not always easy …'

'Hush, Mrs. Morgan, no need to fret. You can be proud of your son. A proper little Sherlock Holmes he is! He and his friends have helped us to lay our hands on a thief who has been involved in a network of deceit and criminal activities that have been masterminded in London itself.' Sergeant Price ended this grand sentence on a note of triumph. Huw stared modestly at his feet and the other children shuffled awkwardly.

'Now I understand that all these children stayed with you last night. I'm told that the little Italian boy will be able to live with his brother when all this matter is cleared up. I shall need to have a word with the young man in question but, in the circumstances, I do not think that charges will be pressed, especially as we shall be able to return the items that went missing. And this one here is one of the O'Sullivans, if I'm not mistaken. He's done well in this matter but he should not be wandering the streets.'

'I'll take him to the children's home this afternoon so that he can be with the rest of his family,' volunteered Mrs. Morgan.

'And I understand that these two are relatives of yours,' said Sergeant Price, indicating Megan and Rhys who were looking increasingly uncomfortable.

'Er, yes,' said Mrs. Morgan, hesitantly, 'they are staying with us during the holidays.'

'Well, please ensure that none of them takes the law into his or her own hands in the future. They could get hurt. I shall leave them all in your very capable care, Mrs. Morgan.'

He beamed around at the group of children, shook Mrs. Morgan warmly by the hand and replaced his helmet. Mrs. Morgan accompanied him to the front door and the children gave a collective sigh of relief.

'It's too late for me to go back to the office now,' said Huw, 'after all, Mr. Thomas is not expecting me so we could go to Penarth and tell Paolo that he does not need to worry about Harry any more.'

'And tell Sarah what has happened,' added Megan.

'Yes, yes,' shouted Luigi, jumping up and down with excitement. 'I go to see brother now.'

'Well, Huw' said Mrs. Morgan, who had come back into the room while her son was speaking, 'I am not happy about you telling Mr.Thomas a lie in order to leave work as he has always been very good to you, but in the circumstances …' She looked at Megan and Rhys.

'I still have some questions I need answering where you two are concerned. All this nonsense about being relatives of ours …'

'But we don't have time to explain it all now,' said Annie, sidling up to her mother and stroking her arm. 'We need to take Joe to the children's home and perhaps first we could all have a bite to eat? We've had a very busy day so far.'

'Very well,' said Mrs. Morgan with a sigh, 'Sergeant Price did seem very pleased with you all. Come into the kitchen and have some lemonade and a slice of cake.'

Chapter 32

A SATISFACTORY CONCLUSION

It was late afternoon by the time Megan, Rhys, Huw and Luigi walked along the cliff-top path in Penarth. They met some men in work clothes heading home from the quarry and then they saw a solitary figure coming slowly towards them.

'Paolo!' exclaimed Luigi and set off at a run. Megan was looking around anxiously for the French artist and his painting.

'He's not here!' she declared.

'Who?' asked Rhys.

'The artist, of course. There's no sign of him!'

Paolo had swung his brother up in his arms and was listening to his brother's excited account of Harry's arrest. Huw had joined them and was adding his explanations. Finally, Huw turned to Megan and Rhys.

'That all seems to have come to a satisfactory conclusion, I think,' he said, smiling contentedly. Then he noticed Megan's distraught face.

'The artist's not here,' she said.

'Well, it's getting late now Megan. Perhaps he's

gone home. You can come back earlier tomorrow and make some enquiries.'

'We could ask the ice–cream seller. He sees lots of people,' Rhys piped up, in a cheery voice.

'Oh, Rhys,' sighed Megan, 'all you think about is food.'

'Yes,' said Paolo, 'Let us go and see Domenico and Chiara. I must tell them the good news.'

Domenico and Chiara welcomed them all enthusiastically into the ice-cream parlour, and were especially delighted to see Paolo. They all began talking earnestly in Italian, with many smiles and gestures.

'If they ever stop, we can perhaps ask about the artist,' said Megan gloomily.

Chiara looked over at them and smiled.

'I am sorry. You do not understand what we are saying. After you come yesterday and say you look for Paolo, Domenico, he think for a long time and he say, 'We need someone to help us – we get old and we have no children.' It's a good business – many customers – and Domenico have plans to open café – sell good coffee and perhaps food too. He is asking Paolo if he like to come and live with us – and Luigi, of course – and learn the ice-cream making.'

'That sounds an excellent idea!' exclaimed Huw.

'So Paolo and Luigi will have a proper home,' said Megan, her anxiety about the artist momentarily forgotten.

'And when you marry your young lady, she will be able to join the business too,' said Domenico, reverting to English.

'We are going to call on her now,' said Huw, 'because we promised to tell her the outcome of our plan.'

'Say to her that my feelings for her have not changed and I hope with all my heart that she still feels the same about me. I must settle everything, then I will go to her father and ask if she may marry me. Domenico says that Luigi can stay here with him and Chiara from now on. I have to go back to the farm tonight to do my jobs there and tell them that I shall be leaving. And I must tell the quarry owner that I have found other work. Then, I shall need to speak to your Sergeant Price, Huw and apologize to Mrs. Probert. So many people to see and explanations to make everything right!'

He smiled, paused and looked at Megan and Rhys.

'How can I ever thank you children!' he said, 'Without your kindness in helping my brother, none of these good things would have happened.'

Chapter 33

IN PURSUIT OF THE ARTIST

When they arrived at Sarah's house, the door was opened before they had time to knock, and her anxious face peeped out.

'Do you have news?' she gasped, 'I have been so worried.'

She disappeared for a second and reappeared carrying her straw hat that she crammed quickly on to her head.

'I will walk along the road with you and you can tell me everything.'

The children recounted all that had happened since they last saw her and Sarah proved to be a suitably receptive and delighted listener, hanging on their every word.

'Well, how can I ever thank you?' she exclaimed, when they had finished and she hugged each of them enthusiastically, right there in the street, causing Huw to blush enormously.

'Actually,' said Megan, 'there is something you may be able to do for us. We wondered if, when you walk on the cliff-top, you have ever seen an artist painting a picture of the view – a French man with a very elegant lady?'

'Oh, you mean Monsieur Sisley. Yes, I know him by sight. He and his wife lodge in the house almost opposite mine. Do you know them?'

'We met them on the cliff yesterday but they were not there today,' said Megan.

'Why do you want to see them?' Then seeing Megan's hesitation, she added, 'I am sorry. I should not be so impertinent. I can accompany you to the house and we can inquire for them, if you wish. I know their landlady.'

'Oh, thank you so much, yes please,' said Megan.

They walked back towards Sarah's house and crossed the road. Sarah rang the door-bell and a young girl opened it.

'Hello, Gwen. Is Mrs.Thomas there, please?'

When she recognized Sarah, the girl smiled and called her mistress, who came bustling to the door.

'Good evening, Sarah. What can I do for you?'

'Good evening, Mrs. Thomas. Are Monsieur and Madame Sisley in?'

Megan's heart was beginning to race. She realized that if the artist appeared, she had no idea what she was going to say to him. 'May we use your painting as a time-machine?' sounded like the request of someone who needed to be locked up in the mad-house. However, she was let off the hook.

'No, they are out on an excursion today and they will not be back until late. What is it that you wanted?'

'We were interested in one of his paintings,' said Megan. 'It's a view from the cliffs. We wondered if he'd finished it.'

'Oh, he has painted a number of pictures of that view,' said Mrs. Thomas. 'He has already sent some of them back to France because he is planning to leave soon.'

Megan's heart sank.

'If you come back tomorrow, he may see you. Although, I think that it would be better if your parents came with you.'

'Thank you very much,' said Megan, 'We'll come back tomorrow then, won't we Rhys?'

'Er, yes, I suppose so,' said Rhys, still unconvinced.

'Yes, do come back tomorrow,' urged Sarah, after they had taken their leave of Mrs. Thomas. 'The time will drag so much until I am able to see Paolo again, but in the meantime,' she added brightly, 'at least I can be of some help to his kind friends who have done so much for us both.'

She said goodbye and stood waving to them until they turned the corner of the road.

'Well,' said Huw, 'it seems that you have completed your task here and have found the way back to your own time. Such a lot has happened in the past four days.'

'Four days!' exclaimed Rhys, 'that means our

school trip will be finished and the rest of our year will have gone back to Aberystwyth.'

'We'll worry about that when we get back,' said Megan, 'if we can survive in Cardiff in Victorian times, we should be able to manage in the present.'

Chapter 34

MORE ENDS TIED UP

When they arrived back at Huw's house, Mrs. Morgan greeted them with a welcoming smile and looked as if she had some good news to tell them.

'We took Joe along to the Children's Home,' she said, 'and saw Molly and the little ones. They are looking well, certainly cleaner and tidier than before. I had not realized what good work is being done there. The Superintendent said that they need another housekeeper as they have taken in so many children recently and when I said that I would be interested in such work, he said that he would speak to the trustees.'

'He said that he thought that Mam would be an excellent person to do the job!' said Annie, proudly.

'So you would not need to take in sewing any more?' asked Huw.

'No, and I would only be required to work there during the day as they have another housekeeper who lives on the premises and is there at night. I would be able to keep an eye on Molly and her family too.'

'I am so glad that you have found such a useful job,' said Huw, kissing his mother on her cheek. She put her arm round him.

'I see now that I have been so wrapped up in my own sadness since your father died that I have not really noticed all the folk who are living in much worse circumstances. It cannot have been a very happy home for you two either but now I feel that I really have the opportunity to do something worthwhile.'

That evening was one of the happiest in a long while. All the day's stories were exchanged over a hearty and delicious meal. When Sergeant Price called by later, he added to the good news as he reported that Mrs. Probert had identified her jewellery and was delighted to have it back.

He had explained to her the important part they had all played in apprehending the criminals, and said that Mrs Probert had no wish to bring charges against the Italian youth, although her husband did not seem so willing to forgive and forget. However, it seemed that Mrs. Probert could be a forceful lady when she needed to be and she got her own way there! She accepted that the young man, who she had taken quite a shine to, was coerced by Harry Jenkins and acted against his better judgement.

'So everything is sorted out,' said Mrs. Morgan with satisfaction, 'I delivered Joe to the Dr. Barnardo's Home and do you know ...? But sit down Sergeant Price – and have a cup of tea, if you have the time. We have just finished our supper.'

'Well, I don't mind if I do, Mrs. Morgan.'

He smiled and nodded at the children and followed Mrs. Morgan into the sitting room, settling himself down in an easy chair.

'You children can run along outside for a while as it's still light,' said Mrs. Morgan, 'while I have a little chat with Sergeant Price. You don't want to listen to me rattling on again.'

The children jumped at this opportunity to escape from adult company and walked across to the wall beyond which lay the mud-flats of Cardiff Bay. Huw and Annie climbed expertly up to sit on top and gave Rhys and Megan a hand up to join them. They all sat swinging their feet and looking across to the headland of Penarth.

'Well, everything is sorted out now,' said Huw, thoughtfully. 'Luigi has found his brother and a home, and Sarah is happy again, and Molly and Joe and the little kids are being looked after well. '

'And don't forget Mam,' put in Annie. 'I've never seen her so happy and contented – not since father died, anyway. And she seems to like talking to Sergeant Price, don't you think? He certainly looked at her as if she took his fancy.'

'Annie!' said Huw, sternly. 'You have read too many silly romantic stories. But come to think of it, he is a widower. His wife died a few years ago.'

'There you are then. Megan and Rhys may have found us a new father too!'

'But we still have to find a way to get home,' said

Megan, 'We shall have to go and look for the painting tomorrow, now that everyone has been helped.'

'But you could always stay here with us,' said Annie, cheerfully. 'We'll have such fun during the rest of the summer and you can come to school with me after the holiday.'

'You know that wouldn't work, Annie,' said Megan sadly. 'We need to go back to our own families. But we'll really miss you and Huw.'

'We'll miss everyone,' said Rhys, 'Luigi, Joe and Molly and the little kids as well.'

'Yes, it would be nice if we could see them again before we go, just to say goodbye.'

'We could go with Mam tomorrow morning?' suggested Annie. 'She has to meet the trustees at eleven o'clock.'

'But she'll start asking us where we're from.'

'Don't worry. This new job will occupy her thoughts now,' said Huw.

'And Sergeant Price,' added Annie, mischievously.

Chapter 35

GOODBYES

Before Huw left for work the next morning, he whispered to Megan and Rhys, 'Come outside so I can say goodbye to you. If all goes well, you may be back in your own century before I come home tonight. I wish I could come with you this afternoon – but I dare not risk losing my job.'

They walked along the road and round the corner. Megan had a lump in her throat and even Rhys looked a little damp-eyed.

'We shall always remember you,' said Megan, hugging him, 'I don't know what we would have done without your help.'

'Well, you never know, perhaps one day I shall be able to build a time-machine like the one in Mr. Wells' book and come and visit you, or find a painting to take me to your time. You had better go back now, good luck.'

They stood and watched him walk away. Before he crossed the road at the next corner he turned and waved and then he was gone. They walked back to the house in silence.

They both felt it. Goodbyes were in the air.

Later, Mrs. Morgan readily agreed to Annie, Megan

and Rhys going with her to the children's home. It was a tall, stone-built house with a notice over the door proclaiming 'Dr. Barnardo's Home for Waifs and Strays'. They were shown into a gloomy front parlour and a grey-haired man dressed in a rather worn black suit came in.

'Ah, Mrs. Morgan, delighted to see you again,' he said, shaking her hand warmly, 'come through to the living-room and I'll send the O'Sullivan children in to see you. Then, Mrs. Morgan, we shall go to my study and meet two of our trustees.'

They went into a brighter room with large windows opening onto the garden where they could hear children playing. A few minutes later the O'Sullivan children came in. Megan and Rhys were taken aback for a moment at the change in their appearance. The girls were wearing plain, neat dresses and clean white pinafores. Their hair had been brushed and tied back with coloured ribbons. Joe looked scrubbed and well-dressed. No-one spoke until the grown-ups had left the room. Then there were many delighted hugs and exclamations.

'It's not bad at all here,' said Joe, 'the grub's really good. I think I could get used to it. And the beds are better than the ones at home.'

'Yes,' said Molly. 'The little'uns are looked after properly here, and I shall be able to go to school again.'

'We've come to say goodbye,' said Megan,

'because we are going home now. We'll never forget how kind you were to let us stay with you and help us to find Luigi's brother.'

'Home?' said Molly, 'I thought you had run away from home. You never did tell us where you'd come from.'

'Huw and Annie will tell you the whole story one day,' said Rhys.

'Well, wherever you're from, you're nice kids,' said Molly. 'And you seem to have had a good influence on Joe – he says he's going to go to school again and not wander the streets any more.'

'I thought it might be fun to read all those exciting stories you told me about,' Joe said, grinning at Megan.

When Mrs. Morgan came back into the room, she was smiling.

'The Trustees say that I can start next week,' she said. 'So, Molly, I shall be seeing quite a lot of you and your brothers and sisters. I never realized that things were so difficult for you,' and to Molly's surprise, she hugged her warmly. 'It all goes to show that you should not judge people too quickly and I am afraid that I was guilty of that.'

Once they were outside in the street, Annie said hastily, 'You don't need to worry about us for the rest of today, Mam. We need to go to Penarth again to see how Luigi is – Huw has given us some money for the ferry – and we promised that we would call on Sarah Bennett, Paolo's fiancé.'

'Well,' Mrs. Morgan said hesitantly, 'I'm not sure that you should go on your own without Huw. And I really wanted to go and visit my friend, Ruby, in Loudon Square this afternoon. I have not been to see her since – well, since before your father passed away and I have so much to tell her.'

'Please let us go, Mam, please,' pleaded Annie, and Megan and Rhys exchanged uneasy glances. This wasn't looking hopeful.

But as they turned into James Street, Rhys noticed a familiar figure running towards them, waving.

'Look,' he said, 'isn't that Huw over there?'

Sure enough, Huw arrived, and out of breath too. 'Mr. Thomas said I can have the afternoon off,' he panted. 'Apparently he'd heard from Sergeant Price that I'd been busy catching criminals, and he thought I had better have the afternoon off to recover so I can come with you to Penarth!'

Megan and Rhys grinned, happy to have his company for a while more.

'Well, in that case, I can go and see Ruby,' said Mrs.Morgan contentedly, 'but first of all, I need to get us something to eat.'

Chapter 36

ON THEIR WAY HOME

The ferry hooted and set off from the dockside. The four friends leaned against the railings and let the breeze ruffle their hair. They gazed across the grey waves at the tall masts and smoking funnels of the ships carrying coal to all the corners of the world. Tugs and ferries steamed busily to and fro and small fishing boats bobbed in the distance. This was surely the last time they would make this journey together.

Although no-one said anything, they were all thinking the same thing. They had had a great time together, an exciting time and now they were good friends; but friends who were separated by time.

The sun came out and glinted on the water and the ferry landed safely in Penarth.

Their first stop was at the ice-cream shop. Luigi came running out to greet them. Overnight he had been completely transformed. His face was clean, he was dressed neatly and his hair had been cut and combed.

'Sarah is here!' he declared, grinning broadly. 'Come! See!'

Inside, Sarah and Ellie were seated at one of the tables each with a dish of delicious looking ice-cream in front of them. Sarah jumped up to welcome them, a radiant smile on her face.

'Ciao, ragazzi, come, children, sit. I give you some of my ice-cream.' Domenico also seemed to be in high spirits.

Rhys glanced at Megan He was very tempted by the offer, but could see that she was anxious to get away.

'Don't forget that we need to see Monsieur Sisley,' she said. As Sarah's smile turned to disappointment, she added hastily, 'But we know where his house is, so you stay here with Luigi and finish your ice-cream. Huw and Annie are coming with us anyway.'

'We'll see you later,' said Huw

And so they said their goodbyes – and very warm goodbyes too, because Megan and Rhys both knew that there was a chance that they wouldn't see these dear friends again.

'Oh dear,' sighed Megan as they walked up the path to the town. 'I wish we could have explained it all to them. It seemed so odd to leave them like that.'

Rhys agreed. 'And we didn't say a proper goodbye and thank you to your mother either,' he said to Huw and Annie. 'She was really kind to us.'

'Never mind, she'll understand' said Annie, 'and perhaps one day we'll be able to tell them all the whole story.'

'But now we need to think about what to do next,' said Rhys, 'like, where are we going to change into our own clothes? We can't go back to our own time looking like this.'

'What about that place where we talked to Sarah the other day? Behind that bench there are some big shrubs, and I'm sure there is a little clearing there where you won't be seen,' suggested Huw

'Good idea,' said Megan. 'And we'll have to put these old clothes over our school ones for the time being and roll up our trousers so they don't show.'

They reached the bench and slipped into the shrubbery while Huw and Annie kept watch. When they emerged a little while later, they looked rather plumper under their two layers of clothing.

'Well, we're ready now,' said Rhys. 'I hope this is going to work.'

And, with their two friends, they hurried on up the hill towards the house which, maybe, held the key to their return home.

Chapter 37

VIEW FROM THE CLIFFS, PENARTH, SUNSET

'Ah good afternoon children. Yes, Monsieur Sisley is in'.

Mrs. Thomas showed them into the parlour. Megan felt hot and uncomfortable with the dress over the top of her school clothes. It was really tight and she couldn't move her arms properly. And to make matters worse, she felt that her rolled up trouser legs were already starting to fall down.

'Ah, here is the young lady who asked me so many questions the other day on the cliff. And you have brought your friends along with you I see.' The artist smiled at the group of children. Megan blushed, her mind went blank and, now that the moment had come, she could think of nothing to say. Rhys also seemed to have been struck dumb. Huw came to their rescue.

'Very pleased to meet you, sir. It is very kind of you to receive us. We would like to look at the picture that you were painting the other day of the view from the cliffs.'

'Yes, I have finished that painting now. Why are you so interested in it?'

There was an embarrassing silence and then Megan said, hesitantly, 'I erm … we … think our grandmother would like to buy it.'

'So, she cannot come herself to see it? She must have great confidence in your good taste, Mademoiselle.'

Sisley chuckled and led them towards the staircase.

As they followed, Megan was full of doubts. Even if the painting was the right one, would it still work if the artist was there with them? After all, they had been alone, except for Mr. Bartholomew, last time it happened. But how would they be able to get rid of him and have the painting to themselves?

They had reached the first landing when the doorbell rang again and they heard Gwen calling Mrs. Thomas,

'It's a Mr. Bartholomew to see Mr. Sisley. Shall I show him into the parlour?'

Rhys and Megan exchanged an excited glance.

'Today, everyone wants to see me,' the artist said, with a shrug. 'I must go and talk to this Monsieur Bartholomew for a moment. But I will not be too long I think. My studio is on the top floor, so if you would like to wait here, I will return shortly.' He gave them a polite nod of the head and made his way back down the stairs.

'You see, Mr. Bartholomew has rescued us,' Megan whispered to the others, 'but I really think we need to be by ourselves for the picture to work.'

Huw nodded, a little sadly, and said, 'I understand. We'll stay here and keep a look out.'

'Good luck!' said Annie, 'We will miss you both.'

They all hugged each other warmly in turn and then, with a last wave, Rhys and Megan scrambled up the stairs as fast, and as quietly, as they could. Voices wafted up from the rooms below and, once, a door slammed nearby, which made them jump. But, in a short while, which felt like an age, they arrived at a small door that led to the attic studio. Stacks of painted canvasses leaned against the walls. Tubes of oils and palettes smudged with different coloured paints were scattered over the table. There was a pungent smell of paint and linseed oil.

'Which one is it?' hissed Rhys, looking round at the choice.

Megan stood rooted to the spot, not knowing which way to turn. Then, Rhys noticed that one painting was resting on a large easel, hidden by a white cloth. He peeked behind it.

'Is this the one?' he asked.

Megan took a look and recognized the painting which they had seen on the cliffs. She pulled the cloth away.

'It is!' she whispered excitedly. 'Quick, before anybody comes. Help me, Rhys.' She was already struggling out of the dress. She stuffed it in her bag and grabbed Rhys by the arm, while he tugged away at his old ragged shirt.

'Come on. I'm sure that Mr. Bartholomew is helping us make our getaway.'

They stood next to each other and looked at the picture. It showed the cliff sloping down to the stony beach and the coastline curving round to Lavernock Point. The tide was out and the scene was bathed in the evening sun.

'Are you ready, Rhys?'

'Ready.'

As they stared at the painting, they felt themselves being drawn towards it. They could still hear voices drifting up the stairs, but they grew fainter as the sound of rushing air increased. They closed their eyes and instinctively clung on to each other's hands as they felt the floor of the attic studio begin to melt away.

Chapter 38

BACK IN THE MUSEUM

When they opened their eyes, they were standing on the polished floor of a gallery in the National Museum, in front of the framed painting of the cliffs at Penarth. They let go of each other's hands in embarrassment and looked around, blinking in the harsh electric light.

'Hey, what are you children doing in here? The rest of your class is downstairs in the natural history galleries.' A museum guide was eying them suspiciously from the doorway of the room.

This was not the gallery that they had been in when they had been sucked into the painting of the docks and for a moment Megan did not know which way to go.

'Your teacher will be wondering where on earth you've got to. It's straight through the next gallery and down the stairs. Hurry up.'

They started to walk towards the next room, still in a daze. The guide sighed and muttered something about 'kids today' as they passed.

'It must still be the same day if our class is here,' said Megan, 'Do I look OK?'

'Yes, you look the same as usual. Your hair's a bit messy but that's all. What about me?'

'Just the same, except that your clothes are all creased up. But it really did happen, didn't it?' She stopped and opened her bag. Annie's dress was still inside.

'Wait a minute,' she said.

She ran back to the attendant.

'Excuse me. Do you know a museum guide called Mr. Bartholomew? A tall man, with white hair?' she asked.

'I can't say that I've ever heard the name but we do have new volunteers from time to time. Now you run along or you'll be in trouble.'

'Thank you.'

She caught up with Rhys. He was peering in his bag.

'Yes!' he said, triumphantly, 'I still have my Victorian cap – the one we got from the nuns. I thought I'd bring it with me in case we have another Victorian Day at school.'

'So it must have all happened. But we won't be able to tell anyone about it because they'll never believe us.'

They raced down the stairs and into the natural history galleries.

'Come along you two. Where *have* you been? The tour has already started,' said Miss Jones, briskly. 'No more lagging behind. You need to pay attention so that you can fill in your worksheets.'

Rhys groaned.

'I thought we might at least have missed that,' he whispered to Megan, 'and what's worse, we finished our packed lunches about four days ago!'

AFTERWARDS

The remainder of the school visit to Cardiff passed without incident. Rhys made sure that he was not left behind again and Miss Jones commented to his parents on how attentive and well-behaved he had been.

Once they returned to Aberystwyth, their memories of their time in the Victorian city gradually faded and seemed unreal. From time to time, when they were on their own, they talked about what had happened.

'I wonder what everyone did after we disappeared,' said Rhys. 'Huw would have had a bit of explaining to do!'

'Don't forget that Mr. Bartholomew was there – he would have helped them. But I hope they were all happy afterwards,' said Megan.

Towards the end of the summer holidays, she went to stay with her grandparents in Penarth and remembered her visits to the Victorian town with Huw and the other children. One afternoon, she went into one of the charity shops with her grandmother. She had a quick glance through the children's book section but there was nothing interesting.

As her grandmother was browsing, she looked around to see what else there was and noticed a box of old, yellowish photographs. Her attention was attracted by the clothes worn by the people in the pictures – they looked like the ones she had seen and worn in Victorian Cardiff. She flicked through the photos and thought she spotted a familiar face. She pulled out a slightly creased and faded picture of a wedding group and immediately recognized the bride and groom. In the centre of the group, smiling happily were Paolo and Sarah. And, there was Luigi dressed in a smart suit, with Domenico and Chiara at his side, and Huw with Annie, Mrs. Morgan and Sergeant Price.

'What are you looking at, Megan?' Her grandmother came over, with some books in her hand, and peered over Megan's shoulder.

'What a lovely photo!' she said, 'If you're so taken with it, I'll buy it for you. It's such a shame that family photos like these end up in charity shops and no–one knows who the people are. But they certainly look a very happy group.'

'Yes, they do, don't they?' said Megan, with a contented little smile.

ABOUT SHEILA...

I was born and brought up in Northampton, but after studying French at university I became a translator for a few years while my three children were growing up. I love languages – perhaps you can detect that from this book!

Later, I became a secondary school librarian in Oxfordshire – and that was a perfect opportunity to read lots of books and meet many interesting authors and poets. Very inspiring!

I also love visiting art galleries and looking at paintings – and I really wanted to write a book which linked young people to the fascinating world of art.

And now I live in Penarth, near Cardiff and am happily settled in Wales. Cardiff is a great capital city and the National Museum there is a place I visit often, and where I volunteer. I hope my novel inspires you to go there too!